HIGHWAY

Donald O'Donovan

Published by Open Books 2011

Cover art "Highway" by Kamil Bartłoszewski
Learn more about the artist at riffo.deviantart.com

ISBN: 0615722857
ISBN-13: 978-0615722856

1

That upright piano in Passaic, I thought by Christ it was going to kill me. We had a piano board, but a piano board won't help you much on a stairway, and besides, one of the wheels was locked. We chipped some corners off the slate steps going up. The young-old lady in her see-through blouse hovered over us. I thought at first she was coming on to me. But no, she just wanted to make sure we did everything right. And that we didn't step on her stinking little Pekingese that kept nipping at my ankles. We inched that piano up those stairs—three flights in all—stopping after only two or three steps. The stupendous weight of the thing was terrifying. Each time, before we hoisted the son of a bitch once again, as Armando's mocking black eyes met mine—"Can't you take it, *guero?*"—I felt tears starting at the back of my throat. I was *afraid* of that piano.

When it was over, Armando suggested going to a "cantina" for a beer. I told him, in Spanish, to kiss my ass. I just wanted to get away from him. I had three thousand dollars—our running money—in my pocket. I didn't give a rat's balls what this wetback from Oaxaca wanted me to do, or what Reggie Ray, our boss, "El Jefe," wanted me to do: I wanted to do what *I* wanted to do. And I held the purse strings.

1

I shucked a few hundred-dollar bills off my Philadelphia bankroll and stuffed them at Armando. I called a cab; I went to a bar and got grandly drunk; I talked with the barmaid for three hours—in my own language, not Spanish. After my night of drunkenness I took a taxi to the Sheraton Hotel.

"Los Angeles, California," the girl at the desk said. "Jerzy Mulvaney, you're a long way from home."

I could never have told my parents that I was a writer. Such a thing would have been unthinkable. If I'd kept the summer job I'd had when I was sixteen, a laborer for the Otsego County Highway Department, that would have been perfectly acceptable. If I'd become a clerk at Augur's Bookstore or Withey's Drugstore, why, that would have been even better, because I would have been working "inside." Or if I'd stayed in the Army…

I know they talked about me behind my back—all of them except Aunt Mizpah. What was the explanation for my vagrant, edge-city lifestyle, and the succession of jobs, the many changes of address, and the brushes with the law? Maybe I was unbalanced.

Certain members of the family, especially on the German side, were unquestionably a little funny in the head, going back to Maddalyn Isolde Shimmersalz, my maternal grandmother, who committed suicide by drinking Paris Green, an insect poison. Then there was Uncle Augustus, who played with paper dolls and spent a summer living in a tree. And my mother, of course, who did a couple of stretches in the nuthouse at Binghamton. In any case, crazy or sane, I was the black sheep, a complete failure and an embarrassment to the family.

Aunt Mizpah, my mother's maiden sister, was the only member of the clan who had the slightest inkling of what I was about. We exchanged long literary letters over the years. Aunt Mizpah had been engaged, as a girl, to a poet, Ashley Van Deerlin, who drowned in Lake Dunmore the day before their wedding. That was when she started on the sauce, my sister Erin and I figured, way back then.

Aunt Mizpah shared some of Ashley Van Deerlin's letters and poems with me. She kept his faded photograph on her dresser as well as his collected poems and love letters, tied with a crinkly lavender bow, as a sort of shrine. She even wrote a poem herself, dedicated to Ashley Van Deerlin, "To a Poet who Died Young." It wasn't very good, as I recall.

"Will you be needing a wake-up call?"

"Yes. No. Yes… What city is this, anyway?"

"Passaic. Passaic, New Jersey."

"Passaic… Yeah, sure, Passaic."

"Are you okay, sir?"

I slept that night in a king-size bed on pink sheets. In the morning, or to be more accurate, in the afternoon, after a sumptuous meal at an Italian restaurant, I again hired a taxi and ordered the driver to cruise around town, looking for a Mercury Movers trailer hooked up to a red and white International cabover with a winged foot logo on the door. At last we found it, parked in back of a Motel 6.

Armando and I had been on the road for two months. All across America the other truck drivers treated us like poor relations because we were bedbug haulers—furniture movers. The truckload company drivers—Schneider, England, Covenant, even JB Hunt—don't touch their freight. For them, it's strictly drop and hook. You drop your trailer at your destination, you pick up another one and you haul ass, nice and clean. You don't unload your trailer. But us poor saps, the bedbug haulers, we have to wrestle with grand pianos, steamer trunks and vintage chrome dinette sets, and that makes us, in their eyes, the lowest of the low.

On top of that, I had cabin fever. I was sick of Armando and I was sick of talking Spanish. He didn't speak a word of English and he refused to try. I had to interpret everything for him, even to the extent of translating the menus in the truck stops, and of course I had to order for him too. Since my Spanish was far from perfect it sometimes happened that I didn't know the correct word and had to express myself in a roundabout way. For instance, I didn't know how to say "speedometer," so I called the speedometer, in Spanish, "the wristwatch of the miles." Toll booths I called "the little houses of paying," a junkyard, "the cemetery of cars," and so on. Instead of supplying the correct word, Armando made fun of me. He constantly remarked that I was "*muy burro*," very stupid, and that my mind was "*basura*," trash.

Like a lot of short men, Armando was a little tyrant. Always we had to do everything *his* way. Although he was domineering, moody, verbally abusive and sometimes even shoved me, I never thought of retaliating physically since I was five inches taller and outweighed him by twenty-five pounds. Instead, I stupidly allowed this lout, this mouth-breather from Oaxaca, to dominate and bully me from one coast to the other.

Now, as I confronted Armando in the motel room, he characteristically assumed the stance of an inquisitioner and began interrogating me. Had I considered that what I'd done might cost both of us our jobs? Yes, I'd thought about it some. And the running money? Yeah, I did spend some of it. And so, what will El Jefe say? El Jefe can say what he pleases. He can charge the money against my salary or he can fire me right now.

As I gazed at Armando sitting on the edge of the bed with a 40-ounce King Cobra balanced on his knee, I realized that my spree at the Sheraton had done little to dissipate the anger and resentment that had been building up in me over the thousands and thousands of miles. I was trembling and I thought to myself: *I'm actually going to take a swing at this motherfucker.*

Armando jumped to his feet and faced me. I thought we were going to tangle ass, but no—instead, he evinced one of his mercurial changes of mood. He grabbed my hand and shook it; he laughed and slapped his thigh. I was a *buen trocero*, he said; he was overjoyed to be running with me; he couldn't wait to get back on the road, and let's spend some more of the boss's money and fuck El Jefe anyway. He was a hard guy to figure, Armando, but one thing I was starting to realize: he liked it when I stood up to him.

El Jefe—Reggie Ray, our boss—was a shuck-and-jive artist, a smooth talker, always a toothpick dancing over his lips. Reggie Ray had a criminal mind. It's possible that he may have done some time. I never asked him, of course. After all, he was my boss, and besides, a guy like Reggie Ray would never give you a straight answer anyway.

Reggie Ray knew the trucking business inside and out. Before becoming an owner-operator and an entrepreneur he'd pulled for Zero Refrigerated out of San Antonio, the reefer-haul. El Jefe was an excellent driver and he knew America—the roads, the towns, the Interstates—as few men do. To Reggie Ray the United States was just one small town.

El Jefe was also an expert packer and loader. Not particularly strong, he had a fine sense of leverage and balance. He knew how to use a dolly and he made innovative use of a hump strap. He showed me, in fact, how to use a hump strap on a king mattress for an easy one-man carry, something I'd never seen or done before.

Reggie Ray was nice looking and enormously personable. He bowled you over at first. But anyone who'd been over the road could see through him in a minute. He spoke with a thick North Jersey accent, which, along with the catchy phrases and the ever-present toothpick, added immeasurably to the sleaziness of his image, the Broadway Sam who promises you a rainbow and leaves you standing on 42nd Street in your skivvies. Still, he was good company on the road; he was a truck driver in his heart. The truth is that even though he was thoroughly dishonest, a manipulator, a flimflam man, a facile and crooked scammer who relentlessly exploited his clients and his employees, I liked Reggie Ray a lot.

The freight-haul drivers and sleeper teams run pretty much on the Interstates, but a bedbug hauler is all over the map. We were constantly on the horn with Reggie Ray all along the way.

"What's your twenty?"

"Billings."

"Okay, I want yez to run over to Rapid City on 90 and load four thousand pounds for Minneapolis and Saint Paul."

There's a logistics to it. For example, if you're running to the east coast and your last stop is New York, but you're also dropping off loads in Denver, KC, Cincinnati, Columbus and Pittsburgh on the way out, naturally you'll load New York in the nose of the trailer, then Pittsburgh, then Columbus, and so on. But it becomes more complicated because you're also picking up new loads en route. Because of this we often had to zigzag or even backtrack. Let's say we were running from LA up to Washington and we had to load six thousand pounds in Portland for Jacksonville, and Tacoma was in the nose, then we'd have to go to Tacoma and unload then double back and pick up Portland.

All this and much more Reggie Ray coordinated in the "Map Room," his office on Santa Monica Boulevard. Mercury Movers was a wildcat trucking operation. Reggie Ray himself was in fact the only man in the company who had a current Class A license. His drivers were illegal aliens like Armando, ex-convicts, men running from the law, and desperadoes like me who would take any sort of work.

At the start of each haul you got your running money. Thus you were assured of eating. On the road it seemed like you were flush, but it was an illusory sort of wealth. That horse-choking bankroll was company money. You had to pay out for diesel, permits, repairs, scales, tolls and the rest of it. When you got back into LA, after being on the road for a month, sometimes two or three, and Reggie Ray did his arithmetic in the Map Room with the calculator, you could easily come out in the hole. So, he'd set you up with another load, hand you your running money, and off you went, running balls out for the other coast. Vassalage is what it was, with Reggie Ray, the Master Scammer, as lord of the manor and his frazzled and sleep-starved drivers as the serfs.

Reggie Ray had six units constantly in operation, the International, three ancient Freightliners, a Kenworth, and a Mack, all of them cabovers, the latter assigned to a special pal of Reggie Ray's, Shawn, the only driver privileged to run solo. There was also a 1973 Diamond Reo conventional, a classic tractor in mint condition, the Rolls Royce of the fleet. This legendary truck was Reggie Ray's personal rig. No one else was allowed to drive it. Although Reggie Ray spent most of his time in the Map Room, every now and then, just to keep his hand in, the Master Scammer would climb up into the cab of this magnificent fire-breathing dragon of a tractor, the great and glorious Diamond Reo, and take a load out, sometimes to the east coast, or more often, so as not to absent himself too long from the Map Room, the short haul or "local" run up to Portland or Seattle.

But the Map Room... To see Reggie Ray ensconced in the Map Room, leaning back in his padded swivel chair and glancing up at the maps and schedules and rosters plastered on the walls—his toothpick dancing in his mouth, cradling a phone to his ear, another telephone blinking on hold, reaching with his free hand for yet another jangling phone—this was to see a man who had found his supreme niche in life. Reggie Ray, in the Map Room, was planted in the absolute live center of the world he knew as well as most people know their own names and addresses: that is, America, the United States, the world of the American road, the towns, the turnpikes, the hubs, the truck stops, the freeways, the crooked and little-known access roads that lead to this or that on-ramp. The great cross-country routes, mostly the Interstates, were highlighted on the wall maps with magic markers of various coded colors. Reggie Ray tracked his desperado drivers, his cross-continental madmen, with color-coded pins and tacks which he moved, on the maps, as his hirelings called in with their "twenties". He was forever on the phone, or two or three at once, hooking us up, Armando and me, and his other drivers as well, with new loads, new destinations. He leaped from the phones to the fax machine to the computer terminal, then to the map, shuffling his chessmen this way and that, with the theatrical aplomb of a great general making momentous battlefield decisions which were certain—at least in his mind—to rewrite the history books.

It was all fluid, mutable, all vacillation and teeter tottering; it was all timing, windows, juggling, fluctuations, synchronicity, an interlocking grid of fleeting opportunities, incredibly intricate and involved. Reggie Ray's genius consisted in his uncanny ability to get everything to coalesce, to balance this exigency against that, adroitly shifting funds from one account to another, making a phantom deposit, buying stocks on margin, floating a loan here, doing a little double-entry bookkeeping there, and deftly covering his tracks with all the dexterity and savvy and seat-of-the-pants sagacity of an old-time thimble-rigger. He had the ability to anticipate, to negotiate, to neutralize, to offset, to stage a diversionary movement on one front only to pop up unexpectedly on another with a new shell game, a new subterfuge, an explosive and audacious display of hocus-pocus and gimcrackery, or a dazzling exhibition of broken-field running. Slippery, gimmicky, endlessly resourceful, classically cool under fire, he'd run up a flag of truce and confront his accusers with a perfect poker face; then, just when it seemed that they had him dead to rights, he'd put his pursuers on a cross-town bus with the shoddiest of his carpetbagger's tricks.

Wherever there was a deal to be made, a wager to be staked, or a hundred-to-one shot to be risked, Reggie Ray was there with his deck of marked cards and his loaded dice and his pirate's instinct for survival. Above all, the quality that put Reggie Ray in the catbird seat was his almost magical ability to outmaneuver, to circumvent, to propitiate, to bamboozle—to cool the moment—then, to use the breathing space thus gained to regroup, to steal a march, and finally, marshalling all of his grifter's cunning and Gypsy horse-trader's skill, to run his opponents into a duck blind.

Disasters did happen. Frequently Reggie Ray's drivers, those who were on the run from the law, were pinched and sent back to the slam; those who were illegal aliens were nabbed and deported. Sometimes a driver would simply up and quit, leaving the rig and the customer's shipment stranded mid-continent. In such a pickle Reggie Ray would often hire a joker off the street or on the basis of a long-distance phone conversation. Thus it was quite possible for a desperate and out-of-work man to bluff his way into the job without having the slightest idea how to handle an eighteen-wheeler. One such driver missed a gear coming down the Grapevine and died along with his co-driver in a flaming wreck that totaled the rig and the shipper's goods. In a similar incident, a novice driver burned up his brakes on Donner Pass and subsequently plunged to his doom. One desperado stole a rig and ran for Tierra del Fuego. Another man, a refugee from Guatemala who was wanted for rape in Kansas, pulled a heist in Rahway, then dropped his trailer and ran bobtail to Miami, where he was charged with armed robbery, assault with a deadly weapon and impairing the morals of a minor. A fellow named Roy, who was quite a gentleman and seemed very knowledgeable about the trucking business, sold one of Reggie Ray's tractors to a chop shop in New

Orleans and hit for the Big Apple. He was arrested at Kennedy International Airport when he tried to board a flight for Paris with a bomb in his suitcase. It was later discovered that he was an escapee from the Atascadero facility for the criminally insane.

These disasters and losses Reggie Ray took perfectly in stride. Strange to say, it wasn't the money that motivated him. The money was necessary to keep the wheels turning, to enable, to lubricate, to facilitate. The money was a means, not an end. It wasn't the money that Reggie Ray loved: it was *control*—control over people's lives, control of the criss-crossing continental movement of his rigs, control of the loads. He didn't care at all if he ran in the red—just as long as he ran.

For Armando and me, at this juncture, the next destination was Coraopolis, outside of Pittsburgh, where we had to drop off a load. When we hit Coraopolis, with me at the wheel and Armando in the sleeper, we couldn't get under the Coraopolis Bridge. There was an eleven-foot something clearance. I woke Armando, he got up cursing, jumped down from the cab in his socks and stopped traffic—a hell of a mess—while I backed up the rig and got us turned around. I parked in front of a 7-11 and went inside. The clerk was busy drawing a map. He didn't look up as I approached the counter.

"You're out there in the cabover?"

"Uh huh."

"And you want to go to Coraopolis..." With a grin he handed me the map.

After we dropped off three thousand pounds in Coraopolis and picked up a cash payment we showered for five dollars each at the Eat and Park Truck Stop on Route #23. I put away a stupendous meal and slept like a baby in the sleeper while Armando was out helling around (it was his turn now). The next day we bought sixty-five cases of Rolling Rock beer with company money after agreeing that we'd put the money back in the kitty once we offed the beer on the shaky side.

Good to go! Loaded with cases of beer and furniture, we hit for Buffalo on I-90. Now that we'd become entrepreneurs the future seemed unexpectedly bright. We were both wearing our Mercury Movers hats with the winged foot logo, and it seemed to me in that moment, as Armando began to talk expansively about what we were going to do after we'd made our mint, that the great god Mercury's winged feet would take me wherever I wanted to go in life, now and forever. Our first destination, according to Armando, would be Oaxaca, Armando's hometown, where I would find a *novia*. The best place for me, he maintained, would be the Santo Domingo Hotel, near downtown Oaxaca, the market and the cantinas, where, Armando assured me, there were girls, and they would go for ten bucks American a night, a bit of news that I found endlessly enthralling.

Yes, I loved this scenario, and for the first time since we'd begun the trip I found myself enjoying Armando's company. It was as if the beer we were hauling in the trailer—the sixty-five cases of Rolling Rock—had watered a garden in the brain of this surly oaf. The shriveled-up pea that normally rattled around inside his cranium had germinated and sprouted and was rapidly becoming a leafy green vegetable with vines shooting this way and that, and everywhere new tendrils and new directions, new horizons. Armando had discovered the world of ideas.

"We will go to Cabo San Lucas," he said in Spanish, perched on the jump seat beside me as I hissed briefly on the brakes to avoid a mower that had veered onto the Interstate. "I have an uncle there who will give us a discount. He works at the Hotel Melia de Cabo San Lucas. The hotel is very big and very beautiful. Good food, plenty of beer and plenty of girls—good girls, and cheap too! *Qué te parece?* We need a vacation, *cuñado*, is it not so? From Cabo San Lucas we can go to Ixtapa, across the Sea of Cortez. It costs very little by boat, my friend. *Y entonces,*

South America—Nicaragua, Costa Rica, Brasil, *quien sabe?* Oh, there are some very beautiful women, amigo, in Costa Rica. And very cheap, *ademas.* You can go to the room there for five or six dollars *de oro.* And so you might wish to leave your novia in Cabo San Lucas—just for a little while—*poco tiempo, tu sabes.* We are *troceros!* We have to be on the road, my friend. *El camino es la vida.* Your *novia* could return to Oaxaca to wait for you. *No te preocupes.* She will give you a promise that she will not go back to the cantinas while you are away. You may be sure of this, *cuñado.* The girls from Oaxaca are very—how does one say?—very sincere. She will not betray you, amigo. And when we leave Costa Rica we will go to Barbados. *Si, mi amigo*, Barbados. Barbados, the Land of Beautiful Women. *Hijole!* The girls there are very *hot*, my friend. Very *hot!* And we are men. Women of Barbados: *calzones abajo!*"

Grim little Rochester. We checked into the seedy Cadillac Hotel on grimy East Avenue in the most frightening quarter of the city, a district that appeared so dangerous that we were afraid to sleep in the truck. After beers and a pizza Armando went with a *Negrita* for ten bucks. In the morning we rolled to the other end of East Avenue, a peaceful residential street lined with Victorian mansions, for our delivery. Then we hit for New Jersey, with Armando at the wheel, to hook up with Shawn, another Mercury Movers driver, for a money-drop as masterminded by Reggie Ray, our boss.

We met Shawn, following Reggie Ray's instructions, at the J. F. Bar and Grill in Haledon, off the 504 turnpike, a foul, smoke-filled centipede's nest in Haledon's one-street barrio. Shawn, an ex-77 Special Forces sniper (as Armando informed me) and an ex-convict (armed robbery), was a very scary dude. Big, strong, scraggly, just drunk enough to be belligerent, he sat at the bar chewing Skoal Bandits snuff and spitting on the barroom floor. On his right bicep was a faded tattoo: *"Death From Above,"* featuring a set of paratrooper wings with a skull in the center. After we'd downed a few beers he began to talk disconnectedly about telescopic sights and infrared scopes and about the faces of the men he'd killed. He spoke only to me, not deigning to even glance at Armando who didn't understand a word of English anyway. I was feeling more than a little antsy in the presence of this professional hit man, and I was afraid to tell Shawn that we didn't have all of the three thousand dollars (the money-drop that Reggie Ray had arranged) because we'd spent a thousand dollars of company money on the Rolling Rock beer.

When Shawn got up to go to the toilet I had a nearly-irresistible urge to simply get the hell out of there. Armando turned to me: "*Qué dice, El Chaun?* What did '*El Chaun*' (Armando's way of referring to Shawn) say to you?"

"Oh, nothing, just talk," I said in Spanish. Then I put the question to Armando: "What the hell should we do about the money?"

"Give *El Chaun* all that we have," Armando said unhesitatingly. "I will talk with El Jefe. Do not worry, amigo. *No te preocupes.*"

Just then Shawn emerged from the toilet and overheard me talking Spanish with Armando. He glanced at me sharply. Clearly he didn't approve.

We had a few more beers. I fingered the roll of bills in my pocket, trying to find the words to tell Shawn that we were twelve hundred bucks short.

"I feel like hammered shit," Shawn said suddenly. "Three days on the road, no sleep, drunk on my ass last night..." He got up off his barstool and, after gracing the barroom floor with a final squirt of brown tobacco juice, went out to his rig to catch some zees.

I felt so relieved that I ordered a double shot of whiskey and the same for Armando.

"*Salud!*"

"You see, amigo? Everything will be all right. *No te preocupes!*"

Armando went to call Reggie Ray with the company card. Always Armando insisted that *he* be the one to wheel and deal with El Jefe (Reggie Ray spoke fluent Spanish but with a heavy gringo accent), which was fine with me but still I had to laugh. Such a self-important little prick, Armando!

When Armando returned to the bar with a grim expression on his mug I thought we'd both been fired—in fact, I was hoping we'd been fired—but, no, Armando had smoothed things over. He didn't tell me how. Reggie Ray was wiring us some jack, but the bad news was that we had to run up to Queens with Shawn and help him unload.

"*Es malo amigo El Chaun*," Armando declared, smacking his fist down on the bar.

We went outside and walked up and down the one-street town of shanty bars and pool halls. In none of these shit-holes did I hear even a single word of English spoken. We ate some beans and tortillas in a nameless taco dive, then wandered into a titty bar. A solitary girl stood on the runway wrapped in a Third Army fatigue jacket. There was no music. We were the only customers. "Want to go to the room for fifteen dollars?" the girl said in Spanish, snapping her gum and without really looking at either of us. We sauntered out.

The next day the wire came in. We were good to go. We divvied up the money with Shawn, as planned, and began the next segment of the elaborate cross-continental itinerary masterminded by Reggie Ray. Armando and I were to run up to Queens with Shawn and help him unload. We'd all come back down to Haledon, and Shawn would run empty to Baltimore where he'd wait for a back load for Jacksonville, New Orleans and Houston. Armando and I would get back in the International and at long and dear last we'd shake the dust of Haledon from our boots. We'd run down to Paterson and Bergen where we'd unload, collect twenty-five hundred bucks, and then we'd shuffle off to Buffalo where we'd load six thousand pounds. Then it would be the backside for us: Cleveland, Milwaukee, Chicago, Denver, Las Vegas and California.

We all piled into Shawn's rig, a Mack Cruise-Liner cabover with a Caterpillar engine and the Mercury Movers winged foot logo on the door. Most of the truckers I know are cautious and even old-maidish drivers, but Shawn was an aggressive and reckless gear-jammer who bullied other vehicles mercilessly, running up on slow or old cars driven by grandmotherly ladies and frightening them half to death with the Mack's gleaming monster grille and the thunderous roar of his Jake brakes. He wore expensive Oakley sunglasses and a Cat Diesel cap—even driving gloves—and he prided himself on using CB lingo, referring to four wheelers, for example, as "roller skates." By way of showing off he went through all nine gears without using the clutch. If a four-wheeler tried to tailgate him, he' deftly flip his tandem duals onto the shoulder, spraying dirt and gravel on the jamoke's windshield. "Fuckin' roller skate... That'll teach him to stay off my ass." That pugnacious little brass bulldog—the Mack trademark, mounted on the Mack's hood—symbolized Shawn's attitude toward everyone on the road and toward the world.

Suddenly we were in New York. Suddenly 42nd Street, Times Square, the Empire State Building, Rockefeller Center and the shutterbugs clustered around the statue of Prometheus stealing fire from the gods.

One of Reggie Ray's rules was, call the customer when you're two or three hundred miles out and give him an ETA. Then you call him again when you're about an hour out to make sure he's going to be home. If he's not home, and you pull up expecting to unload, it could mean expensive—for Reggie Ray—downtime.

We barreled through the Queens Midtown Tunnel, about an hour away from the address on 94th Street. I was hungry enough to eat road kill. I didn't dare say anything, but fortunately for me, Shawn pulled into a truck stop off the Long Island Expressway and we ordered a big spread. It was a palatial joint with a "Professional Drivers Only" section and telephones at your table, and Shawn picked up the phone and called the customer: "Hello, Mr. Grayson? This is Shawn, your long-distance driver. How are you today, sir? Good, that's good to hear. Well, sir, I'm about an hour and a half away from your residence, sir. Will this be a convenient time..."

I couldn't keep from laughing aloud when I heard Shawn rap off this shtick. Shawn and Reggie Ray were cut out of the same cloth, I realized. Either one could have charmed the pants off a Carmelite Nun.

But this telephone conversation was by no means the end of Shawn's astounding transformation. He removed his Cat Diesel cap, combed his hair, shaved off three days worth of beard, and put on a clean T-shirt. With his clipboard tucked under his arm he looked like a fresh-faced college boy. He was angling, of course, for a tip, and damned if we didn't get it—a nice one too, seventy bucks apiece. He knew how to come on to people; he knew how to hide his predatory nature under a sparkling camouflage of manners and kiss-ass talk, but underneath it all he was a career criminal, a man who didn't give a rat's ass about other people, and all of this because at the very bottom it was himself that he didn't respect, it was himself that he hated.

I made a call myself—from a phone booth so Shawn wouldn't hear—to my best friend and former co-driver Roddy Joplin, the essence of which was, *what's cooking?* It had been a while. Roddy's fourth marriage had recently collapsed, I learned, but he was clean and sober and he was running for Thorwaldsson Trucking out of Clear Lake, Iowa, down to El Paso and Del Rio. And the good news was that he had a spot for me. I've never been the sort of a sailor who jumps ship the minute the water gets rough, but this trip with Armando was way beyond the call of duty. "I won't decide now," I told myself, "but if it gets worse, maybe once we get over toward the midwest…"

Back on the road with Queens and Shawn and Haledon at last behind us, Armando checked in with Reggie Ray and reported that El Jefe wanted us to go to Toronto after we picked up Buffalo, then over to International Falls, Winnipeg and Saskatoon, Saskatchewan.

"Fuck this," I said in English. "I won't do it."

We ran up to Pittsfield, a tranquil little town, parked at a Wegnan's and bought some sliced ham, bread, tortilla chips and some Genesee Beer. Armando had another pow-wow with Reggie Ray. Now the Master Scammer was talking about us running up to Fairbanks after Saskatoon.

"I'm going to sleep."

Armando was beginning to realize that when I talked English I meant business. He was becoming cautious around me, which I liked. He understood that I was on the verge of mutiny, that he might soon be stranded in the middle of a strange land without his co-driver and interpreter.

We both slept that night instead of rolling, me in the sleeper and Armando on the doghouse, then we drove to a truck stop for a leisurely breakfast. By an unspoken agreement we were now on a sort of sit-down strike. We were punishing Reggie Ray by indulging in some serious downtime, which was costing El Jefe money. As I started in on my third cup of coffee, I was feeling pretty good. A subtle shift in the balance of power had occurred: I now had the drop on Armando and even quite possibly on the Old Schlockmeister himself.

Armando, looking worried, went to make another call. A few moments later he returned and approached our table gingerly, almost respectfully.

"*Qué dice El Jefe?*" I barked. "What does he say, the Boss?"

"We will go to Fairbanks."

"In a pig's ass we will!"

I dug my Mercury Movers calling card out of my wallet

and marched to the phone. I would give Reggie Ray an ultimatum: either we'd do the New York turnaround as planned, or I'd take my fair share of the running money and get on a Greyhound bus and Armando could run alone to Toronto and Saskatoon or Fairbanks or wherever.

I could imagine Armando's reaction. I mean, if I decided to bail on him. *Where will you go, amigo?* Where will I go? New York, for one, amigo. Back to LA. It wasn't as if I didn't have options. I could join Roddy Joplin in Clear Lake. Or maybe I'd drop in on my Aunt Mizpah in Vermont. Not unannounced, of course. But I knew she'd be glad to see me.

But, as things turned out, I didn't have to deliver my ultimatum. The Canada-Alaska leg had fallen through, Reggie Ray informed me right off the bat. The timing was wrong, the shipper wasn't ready, or something. At least that's what he said. But the truth is that he probably heard something in my voice that told him this time I wasn't jiving. Reggie Ray knew when to back off. He knew when to go back to his own corner and do some quiet shadow boxing while he waited for his opponent to make a fatal mistake. They didn't call this bastard the Master Scammer for nothing.

"You guys hit for Buffalo and I'll see yez in a few days. And keep it between the ditches, okay?"

In Buffalo, we did another money drop and met Reggie Ray's newest driver, M'Butu from Mogadishu, a hulking Ethiopian with a livid scar across the bridge of his broad flat nose. Supposedly, he'd escaped from a Somali prison, but nobody seemed to know much about the guy. He had no English, and besides that M'Butu from Mogadishu wasn't the sort of man you would want to question about his personal life.

Life seemed good as we turned and headed for the Shaky. There was nothing to do now but steer and gear. I felt as if I really did have wings on my feet. Miles and miles of cornfields on I-90 as we cleared Cleveland and Lake

Erie and rolled for Milwaukee and Chicago at night, the great city spitting fire into the sky, and tolls, tolls, tolls. "*Le vale verga*," Armando commented. In Melrose Park we pulled up to sleep in front of a Lucky Dog, and in the morning there was a Monarch butterfly perched on our hood.

The Bar-B Truck stop in Des Moines, a shower and a buffet, hog prices on the radio, eight hundred seventy miles to Denver, seventeen hundred to LA. My thighs and biceps were black with bruises from loading and unloading. At Grand Island on I-80, marker 305 at a 76 Truck Stop, we took on a hundred gallons of diesel, then stuffed ourselves at the buffet: $7.95, all smilingly watched over by the good prairie-mother waitresses.

A stop at the Detco Truck Plaza in North Platte for coffee, then we rolled in divine silence with Armando at the wheel and me in the jump seat beside him with my mental tachometer turning over at a steady 1,600 rpms. I was feeling mellow, and I was no longer thinking about jumping ship and joining Roddy Joplin. I liked running with Armando when he kept his trap shut.

It was Armando, needless to say, who broke the silence.

"*Cuñado.*"

"*Qué cosa?*"

Armando triumphantly held up a pair of sunglasses— Shawn's pricey designer Oakleys. He flashed a brilliant grin.

"*Chinga tu madre, El Chaun!*"

We laughed and laughed. We were starting to have fun together.

Just before the I-76 turnoff for Denver, a deer ran across I-80, sleek and graceful, like a unicorn escaped from some medieval myth, leaping and bounding into a green pasture as dusk's long shadows fell on the Interstate.

At Monarch Pass on I-70 we broke over the Continental Divide—"over the hump"—and began our descent toward Grand Junction and the Pacific Ocean. We crawled across Biblical Utah into pelting rain, past huge mesas, castle-like rocks, red earth and heat steaming up from the asphalt. Alone with the shifting gears, listening to the stacks, with Armando blessedly out of commission in the sleeper, I tried and tried to think of the Spanish word for "rainbow." Could wake Armando. But no, let sleeping dogs lie.

At the I-15 turnoff near Sulphurdale, I pulled into a roadside rest stop. I was weary. I just wanted to conk out for a minute. I tried to settle down, but it was impossible. In my mind I saw trees and bridges flying by, all the miles I'd driven, lights of roadside diners and grease-dive cafes winking like enormous sex-crazed eyes. The American continent was a stupendous barge encrusted with the barnacles and moss of a billion years, while on deck roadside beer signs blinked and hamburgers sizzled on the grill and truckers pressed the pedal to the metal, boosting brilliant showers of sparks into a soft velvety sky. I tried to go to sleep, but the demonic vision wouldn't disperse. Every time I closed my eyes I was back in the thick of it, out on the blacktop, kicking the clutch, jamming through thirteen gears, breathing fumes of burning rubber, jockeying for position with all that streaming mechanical life.

Finally, the shimmering neon mirage of Las Vegas, a posh 76 Truck Stop with phones at the tables, real iced tea and dozens of slot machines. On my first pull I hit a hundred forty bucks on a quarter and quit right there. Armando lost ten dollars but then got it back and picked up another ten. He was in a jolly mood as we sauntered out to the rig.

"*Los Seventy-sixes son muy buenos troc-estopes.*"

We highballed for Los Angeles with Armando at the wheel and me in the jump seat. I felt happy. Armando was talking about Oaxaca again—the Hotel Santo Domingo, the *novia* I would find, our open-ended trip to Costa Rica and beyond—just a poor truck driver's wet dreams, but it sure felt right to me. After we crossed the State line—"Welcome to California"—Armando pulled into a truck stop and I went inside to get us some coffee.

When I came back with the coffee a Border Patrol van was parked by our rig with the lights blinking. The storm troopers had Armando in custody. They were ushering him into the van. There was nothing I could do except climb into the International with my coffee and head for Los Angeles on I-15, kicking the clutch, grinding the gears. *You win this time, my friends, but he'll be back, my desperado from Oaxaca. You can count on that.*

On Santa Monica Boulevard, lined with transvestites in mini-skirts, I stopped at Mercury Moving and Storage to pick up a lumper. I had to unload in Santa Clarita and sell off the sixty-five cases of Rolling Rock. Then I ran back down to LA empty, and after a stop in a barrio near MacArthur Park to drop off my lumper, I parked once again at Mercury Movers. *Thank God!* It was over. I'd been out for three months, to the day. My wages, I estimated, after I turned in my diesel receipts, scale receipts, toll tickets, etc., and Reggie Ray performed his devastating magic with the calculator, would come to about eighteen hundred dollars—not much for three months on the road, but then most of my meals had come out of the running money and I'd picked up a few bucks on the beer deal plus a hundred and forty in Vegas.

After Reggie Ray and I had gotten all the business settled I went out and dropped the trailer and ran bobtail to a fried chicken joint to pick up some dinner for us—on Reggie Ray, of course. I could see what was coming. The Master Scammer, by this small and seemingly generous act, was sweetening me up for the kill. Everything Reggie Ray did had a purpose. But, inwardly, I was adamant. I was off the road and I intended to stay that way.

Over dinner and beers in the Map Room, Reggie Ray

and I discussed Armando's arrest and deportation. Reggie Ray assured me that he'd be wiring Armando money to buy his way back. There was a crossing now in Arizona, over toward Douglas and Agua Prieta, where it would be easy to get across once the money was in place.

"He's a good man, Armando," Reggie Ray said.

"Yes, he is."

As soon as we'd finished eating I handed Reggie Ray the keys to the International.

"Jerzy, as you know, I'm a driver short—"

"Reggie Ray, it's been a slice of heaven, but..." I was serious. I had to get off the road. I was ready to settle down. Maybe I'd get out of LA entirely. I'd go to New York, or maybe I'd even join Aunt Mizpah in green Vermont.

But Reggie Ray had my number. He made me the following offer: I would do the Fairbanks haul—San Francisco, Eugene, Portland, Seattle, Tacoma, Vancouver, Fairbanks and Anchorage, and I could run solo, like Shawn. I'd get an allowance to hire lumpers, a bigger food allowance, and he'd up my wages. I'd have a full week of downtime in Anchorage, expenses paid, hotel and all, while I waited for a backhaul. And I'd be back in LA, considerably richer and off the road for as long as I liked, in less than a month. It sounded pretty good. But Reggie Ray had still another rabbit in his hat: I'd be taking the Diamond Reo conventional, Reggie Ray's personal rig.

Reggie Ray knew human nature, and he knew me. He knew perfectly well that I was primarily a writer, not a career trucker, but he also knew that I wasn't running just for the money, and that I was enough of a truck driver that I couldn't turn down a chance to drive a legendary Diamond Reo to Anchorage.

Reggie Ray held out a fat envelope with my name on it. "Here's your running money." Deftly shifting his toothpick, he flashed that sensational grin of his. "Take good care of my baby!"

2

I was eight years old when the men in white jackets came for my mother, exactly like in the movies. There were two of them. My mother and I were in the kitchen. I snatched up a butcher knife. I would have stabbed the guy in a minute, but the other thug grabbed me. It was one of those long winters in Cooperstown. We were practically snowbound. The wind howling, my mother howling. She was raving, I admit it. The snow was almost up to the eaves. It was dangerous to go out at night. There was a pack of feral dogs on the loose. They devoured an elderly farmer at an isolated farm out near Fly Creek. Ate everything but his feet. You wondered how they could crunch up the bones. Then we learned that the leader of the pack was a bullmastiff. They shot him later. The State Troopers came and my father went out with the posse. They opened the brute up—the same way I would have opened up that funny-farm stooge—and he had the farmer's wedding ring in his belly.

The doctors put my mother on thorazine. That was their idea of therapy. A nice little chemical lobotomy. They make a harmless vegetable out of you.

In Cooperstown, nobody went to a shrink. It simply wasn't done. And there was no such thing as ADHD or schizophrenia or bipolar or any of that. When it came to mental aberrations, there were three categories: Foolish, Funny in the Head, and Not Right.

"Foolish" meant severely retarded, like Lummy Haverhill, the official Village Idiot. "Foolish" was even considered a blessing of sorts, because if you were foolish you were clear of the clockwork. You were on permanent vacation, so to speak, and not subject to the usual trials and tribulations of life. "Funny in the head" meant anything from odd or quirky to mildly insane. There were any number of people in Cooperstown who were funny in the head, and some of them, including my mother, had spent some time in the lunatic asylum down in Binghamton. "Not right" was more serious. If you said, "He's not right," or "She's not right," it probably meant that the unfortunate person had a serious physical defect as well as a mental aberration, and would probably never be "right." The pronouncement "not right" was typically delivered with a rueful shake of the head, as if to say, "Damn shame, isn't it?"

Billy Stamford lived on my street, Pioneer Street, next door to Craven's Taxi and across the street from my best friend, Turk Monahan. Billy was younger. He wasn't foolish or anything like that, just a little slow. His big sister, Selena, was a cleaning lady at the Mary Imogene Bassett Hospital. Their father had been killed at Heartbreak Ridge. Billy, Turk and I would walk to the Frog Hollow Grocery Market, just down the street, for orange Popsicles just about every day, and sometimes, on a hot summer day, if we had the money, the three of us would traipse downtown to Withey's Drug Store on Main Street for a malted milkshake. Withey's was the only place in town where you could get a malted milkshake. A milkshake was one thing, but a *malted* milkshake was something else again. You could get a milkshake at the Doubleday Restaurant, sandwiched between Smalley's Theater and Doubleday Field, or at the Cooperstown Diner on Main Street. But only Withey's had malted milkshakes.

The Stamfords, Billy and Selena, didn't keep any big knives around the house—for a good reason. Billy Stamford's mother, some years back, had hacked Selena's baby daughter to death. That was when they carted her off to Binghamton. They figured she'd been chopping cabbage with a meat cleaver when she went berserk. Bill Rassmussen, the town cop, found her wandering down by the River Bridge, crazy as a betsy bug, with the meat cleaver still in her hand and her apron all splotched with blood. There was no sign of the baby, but they found one of her booties on the chopping block in the kitchen along with some bloody chunks of cabbage. Then a month later, in the dead of winter, Paul Greenfield from the County, fishing through the ice, got something on one of his tipups. He pulled it up and there was the little Stamford baby, frozen solid as a rock.

A few doors past Withey's, up toward Smalley's Theater and next to the Five and Ten, was a scorpion's nest called the Glimmerglass Bar and Grill—the "Glim"—which had the reputation of being the most God awful hellhole in Otsego County. On any given afternoon, as you strolled past the Glim, you might see Rory Goodnight, the drunken house painter, come pitching out the door in his paint-spattered overalls and paper hat, hiccupping and blinking like an owl, reeling in the sunlight, and maybe about that time old Ambrose Clark would come clippity-clopping along in his one-horse shay, tossing silver dollars to cheering village children—old Ambrose Clark, the Village Patriarch himself—with a jovial nod and a wave and a crack of his whip for us all and a hearty, "*Hello, Rory!*"

The Glim was the sort of place you didn't want to go to unless you'd had a couple of drinks beforehand. That way, when you walked in, you saw joyous men and women rollicking and raising their glasses, joking, shouting excitedly at one another, trouping to the jukebox, laughing uproariously for no reason at all, celebrating life, living in the moment. But if you walked in cold sober you saw the poverty and the despair and the lonely, desperate people intent on catching a buzz because they had nothing else to live for. The Glim was the working people's bar, the lower class and below, the street folk, the derelicts, the insane.

But the Glim also had a chic aspect to it, in that the rich folks had recently discovered its quaintness and began dropping in. Honey Haverhill, in her country club tennis sweater, and her husband Darren, with his yachtsman's cap and his glowing tan, might pop in for a drink; or Todd Darlington and his beautiful wife Cornelia, née Vladimirovna, daughter of Colonel Vladimir Andreyev, whose great grandfather was a hero of the Crimean War. If you were one of the Four Hundred, you might have your photograph taken at the Glim in your Russian Lynx fur coat, hoisting a dry martini. Your picture would be published in the town newspaper, *The Freeman's Journal,* and might reach as many as two thousand readers. This photo would signify that you identified with the lower classes, that you shared their suffering, that you willing to walk the sod with the unwanted.

On the way back up Pioneer Street you'd pass the Pioneer Grill, Cooperstown's most popular bar, and here you might see Lummy Haverhill, the Village Idiot, lingering outside with his hand in his pants and a gleaming drool of spittle dangling from his lower lip, while inside Bill Rassmussen, the town cop, would be standing at the bar hoisting a foaming schooner of beer. And frequently by Bill's side, with a boilermaker or a whiskey, the handsome and charismatic Garth DeGrace, whose paintings hung in the Smithy Gallery next door to the Pioneer Grill. And on any given day, if it was mid-afternoon, Garth Degrace would almost certainly have himself a snootfull, and the two of them, he and Bill Rassmussen, would be singing Down East sea chanteys.

If you felt like going the long way home you could walk

Main Street toward the Baseball Museum and go through the little park behind Guido's Market where you'd pass Cooperstown's Man of Destiny with his scarf and his cane and his greatcoat, the giant bronze of James Fenimore Cooper, or "JFC," as we called him, seated on his marble pedestal, gazing confidently out over Cooperstown, *his* Cooperstown, while dozens of strutting pigeons splooped streaks of white down his towering stovepipe hat.

Turk Monahan and I, when we were little, used to climb on that statue nearly every day, and we often sat in JFC's lap. I explored by touch every surface of the bronze giant, the Great Man's huge gloved hands, his knees, his sturdy cane, his greatcoat, the lapels, the scarf, the strong dour features of the man, his bushy eyebrows, the shock of hair, the jaunty top hat.

One day Turk Monahan fell off JFC's statue and broke his collarbone. I couldn't get over how neat and clean it was, comparatively speaking, breaking your collarbone, I mean. I'd broken my arm when I was six and it was a nasty business. But a collarbone, that was a piece of cake, at least for Turk Monahan.

One place in Cooperstown we never went to was the Baseball Hall of Fame, on Main Street, next door to Guido's Market. Nobody from Cooperstown went there. The Baseball Hall of Fame was for the tourists, for the summer people with their expensive cameras and their color-coordinated outfits and their city ways. It was their place, the Baseball Hall of Fame. We never went there. One didn't. You didn't go there. It simply wasn't done.

The Frog Hollow Grocery Market was a wonderful place where you could buy Popsicles, Fudgesicles, Creamsicles, penny candy and other delights from Mrs. Giordano, "Mrs. Gio," who kept a supply of complementary caramels stuffed in the pocket of her store apron. And if you were a few pennies short, it never mattered. "*You pay tomorrow.*" I felt very much at home at Mrs. Gio's. She treated us kids like family.

She sold bait, too; night crawlers. There was a little landing out back where, in the days before the Frog Hollow swamp was drained, we'd sit and dangle our feet in the cool water and listen to the frogs croak. You could fish there too, for bullheads, mostly.

I loved to peer into Mrs. Gio's deli counter at the round, glistening olives, the hardboiled eggs, the salami, the liverwurst and the prosciutto. Everything looked delicious, especially when accompanied by the smell of Italian cooking that drifted from the back of the store where Mrs. Gio lived with her daughter, Lucia, "Mad Lucy."

Mad Lucy Giordano was funny in the head and possibly also not right. Mad Lucy was a Cooperstown icon. It was my father, in fact, who named her Mad Lucy. Whenever there was a thunderstorm Mad Lucy would stand on the landing behind the store singing the *Questa o Quella* aria from Rigoletto at the top of her lungs, and my father would say, "There goes Mad Lucy!"

Mad Lucy rarely, if ever, left the Frog Hollow Grocery Market. She had her own little shanty in the back where she spent most of her time. The place had been a tool shed when Mr. Giordano was alive. Mad Lucy Girodano was reputed to have psychic powers. You went to her door and she let you in and told your fortune with a Tarot deck. Because of this, Mad Lucy was also called "the Gypsy Lady." It was widely rumored that certain young men in town went to Mad Lucy's door for another reason, but I was too young to know for sure whether or not that was true.

One night I was walking home from the movies and got caught in a peach of a thunderstorm. When I got to Frog Hollow I heard singing, and when lightning flashed I saw Mad Lucy standing on the landing in the torrential downpour, with her wild hair streaming down over her shoulders, shaking her fist at the sky and raging at the storm.

For a while, Mad Lucy had a husband of sorts. "The Frog Prince", we called him. He was a handsome young man with a mustache and a shaggy mane of jet-black hair. We'd see him standing on the landing behind the store, leaning on his cane, gazing out at the swamp. He never spoke to anyone, and after a few months he vanished.

There was a story, widely believed on Pioneer Street, that Mad Lucy had found him, the mystery man, badly wounded and unconscious—a Gypsy or an escaped convict—drifting in a rowboat. And that she'd nursed him back to health and took him as her lover.

Another story referred to Mad Lucy's supposed supernatural powers. She'd conjured him up, the Gypsy Man. He was her demon lover. Or else, by means of black magic, she'd changed a bullfrog into a man, and he, the mystery man, the Gypsy Man, was Mad Lucy's prince, her very own Frog Prince.

The story had it that Mad Lucy's Gypsy Man, the lover who disappeared, was supposedly buried in an unmarked grave in the little cemetery behind the Catholic church on Elm Street. The story was that whenever there was a full moon Mad Lucy visited her lover's grave, bringing with her a live bullfrog from the Frog Hollow swamp. The Gypsy Lover then rose from the dead and somehow into the bullfrog's body, and the two of them danced the night away in the cemetery by the light of the moon. It was just foolishness, of course; nobody believed the story, but one day Turk Monahan and I found a big dead bullfrog in the cemetery and we figured he either got too far away from the water or else he'd danced himself to death.

Bill Rassmussen used to say that you could sooner catch a weasel asleep than walk down Cooperstown's Main Street and not see Lummy Haverhill. You'd Lummy Haverhill every day, slouching in front of the Glim or the Pioneer Grill, or sometimes in front of Smalley's Theater. Lummy Haverhill, like Mad Lucy, was a Cooperstown icon. Incredibly, this misshapen oaf was the scion of one of Cooperstown's richest families. He was the brother of Darren Haverhill, whose finely chiseled features often graced the society page of the *Freeman's Journal*. Lummy would go around to the bars, the Glim and the Pioneer Grill. He knew how to order a glass of beer, and that was about all. He couldn't carry on a conversation. Of course he didn't have to worry about money.

Some people might contend that the Haverhill family was heartless and irresponsible to let Lummy wander around town, that such a creature should have been placed in an institution where he could be cared for. But Cooperstown itself was in fact such an institution. Lummy Haverhill was free to roam, and everyone knew him and looked out for him. No one would have dreamed of doing him the slightest harm.

People said that Lummy Haverhill didn't have sense enough to come in out of the rain, which was true, but I often thought that maybe Lummy knew something the rest of us didn't. Lummy loved the rain. It was special to him, somehow. Lummy adored the rain. Every time it rained, he'd rejoice, like a robin or a frog. The heavens would open and he'd try to catch the drops in his mouth. In April or May, when a warm spring rain was dimpling the still surface of the lake, you'd see him standing on the River Bridge, kissing the sky, joyfully greeting the raindrops that came sluicing down, his mouth wide open like a buttercup. He'd roll his eyes and babble, drenched, the rain streaming down his face. You couldn't tell what he was saying. It came out of him like a rhapsody, half formed words, ragged moaning, baby talk almost, crazy gibberish, mumbo-jumbo, reckless, wild.

In Cooperstown the bells of the redbrick Catholic Church on Elm Street counted off the hours, day after day, like a metronome, and the Sawmill whistle blew at five o'clock, week after week, summer after summer, while cicadas droned high in the elms. You went into Withey's

Drugstore on Main Street and you saw the village ladies sitting at the cool marble counter in their summer dresses, sipping their cherry Cokes, and it was as if the prattle that spewed out of their mouths was creating Cooperstown out of their spit and the sound of their mingled voices, creating the leafy neighborhoods and the church steeples and the whitewashed, toy-like houses, creating the docile villagers coming and going in the quiet streets like miniature figures in a child's sandbox.

Then you walked out of Withey's Drugstore and stood on Main Street, and you were one of them, one of those tiny figures. You heard the cicadas droning high in the trees and the drowsy lullaby of the humming telephone wires, and then you heard the five o'clock whistle blow down at the Sawmill and you knew, you knew in your heart, that no one in Cooperstown would ever drink the dragon's blood or descend into the belly of the whale. No one would ever do anything, anything at all. This was the life of the little day, the eternal Cooperstown presided over by James Fenimore Cooper with his top hat and his cane and his bronze greatcoat with its showy epaulets of clustered cooing pigeons. *The eternal Cooperstown*, this everlasting sunlit tableau, this picture-postcard town where the church bells tolled away the hours and the graveyards waited and nothing ever *happened*.

It was enough to drive anyone insane, enough to make you want to pray that they'd come for you and pack you off to the bughouse. I visited my mother at the asylum in Binghamton when I came home on leave from the Army and was astonished at how beautiful everything was. A three-story Gothic Revival style building (now a National Historical Landmark) with massive towers, turrets and buttresses, it looked more like a grand hotel than a lunatic asylum. Spacious grounds, a bandstand and a bell pavilion. I fell in love with the place. I wanted to move right in. Just imagine, what a life! When I closed my eyes it was easy to envision myself among them, playing croquet on an absinthe-green lawn with a few of my fellow lunatics—the men in their tennis whites, the ladies with their parasols—and everything so pruned and pristine and *pointilliste,* as if madness itself were a picnic on Grand Jatte Island. I don't suppose I have to add that I permitted myself to imagine that there would also be a girl in the picture, a soul mate, a mad girl with a shining mind, my very own crazy-beautiful Emily Dickinson.

My second summer job was working at Guido's Market. I put up stock and went on deliveries with the other stock clerk, my neighbor, Vic VanZandt. The stock work was dull enough, and Guido, my father's long-time pal and golfing partner, called me "Young Rufus," after my father, Rufus Mulvaney. Or more often, he simply called me "boy". But the part of the job I liked was on Sundays when I got to go in the truck with Pete, Guido's partner, to New York City to buy produce.

Our rig was a red Freightliner conventional and the lettering on the cab read, "Guido's Market, Cooperstown, New York". Pete kept the tractor parked at his house on Fair Street. We left out early. I'd go to bed at 7:00 p.m. and set my alarm for 3:00 a.m. I'd wear my work shoes and I had a Kenworth hat that I bought at the Mobil Truck Stop at Plattekill on one of our first trips to New York City.

I'd meet Pete at our tractor at 4:00 a.m. His house on Fair Street was crosslots from mine. Pete, freshly shaved, smelling of Bay Rum, his hair slick and black as a seal's fur and glistening with Three Flowers Brilliantine, would have already been up for hours. An early riser, Pete was always the first one to arrive mornings at Guido's Market.

When we first started running to New York, Pete explained to me everything he did for his pre-trip inspection, like checking the brakes and lights and building up his air. When we'd get down to Guido's Market on Main Street, Pete made me get out of the cab and watch him back under the trailer and check to make sure that the jaws of the fifth wheel were locked around the kingpin. He warned me about the danger of a high hook and told me what could happen if you got a trailer separation. Then we'd both walk around our rig while he spanked the tires with a lug wrench and we checked the adjustment on the trailer brakes.

There wasn't a soul around on Main Street when we left out at 4:30. The whole town was asleep. We'd cross Pioneer Street, turn left on Chestnut and roll out on State Highway #28 down to Oneonta, where we'd pull into the Red Barrel Truck Stop for breakfast. There was a big sign that said "PROFESSIONAL DRIVERS ONLY," and we'd put away a huge breakfast: three eggs, ham and sausage, dollar pancakes with real maple syrup, and orange juice and coffee.

Pete's real name was Pietro Bellino, but he was called Pete Bell. Most of the Italians in Cooperstown had anglicized their names. Or the community did it for them, by way of pronunciation. Brunelli became Brown, Abruzzio became Bruce, Bellino became Bell, and so on.

The ragman's name was Vincenzo Martino, but everyone called him Vinnie Martin. He was Pete's cousin. Vinnie Martin went from house to house collecting rags. He lived out on Beaver Meadow Road. His old pickup truck looked like a feather bed made out of rags, billions of rags bedded in the truck and the bulge of them roped down. He'd come to your door and ask to see the lady of the house. "Hello-a dere, Missus. You gotta da rags-a today?"

Vinnie Martin had a daughter, Marisa "Marcie" Martin. She was my age. Marcie Martin had a soft, dark, melting look, as if she were made out of maple sugar.

While we were eating breakfast at the Red Barrel Truck Stop, Pete would talk about the particulars of what we'd buy that day, how many boxes of lettuce, how many bushels of corn and how many flats of strawberries, and so on, and how we'd get the produce ready for display when we got back to Cooperstown. It was clear that Pete was grooming me for the future, that he assumed I would always be working at Guido's Market, that it was my manifest destiny, in fact, and that I would one day take over his job as produce manager.

On the road, Pete was a good driver. I had complete confidence in him. One thing that mystified me at first was the way he shifted without the clutch. I'd always heard that you had to double clutch when you drove a tractor-trailer. Pete explained to me that shifting without the clutch was something you did only after you had been driving for some time and you'd learned to judge when to shift by the sound of the engine. And also that it's a much smoother shift than you get by using the clutch. Later in life, when I went over the road, I discovered that what Pete had told me was true.

It was exciting, rolling into the great city very early in the morning, with Pete sweating and going through the gears, hitting all the lights just right, smiling and glancing at his watch: "We made-a good time, boy."

We'd cross Houston Street and barrel through Little Italy. Traffic would still be light and there'd be hardly anyone in the streets. When we'd get down to Canal Street—Chinatown—there'd be dozens of rigs like ours, and more pulling in all the time, trucks whose sides were painted with signs like, *"Caravaggio and Son, Utica, New York; Fabio Rizzardi and Sons, South New Berlin* and *di Cipolla Grocery Market, Binghamton, New York."*

We'd be munching pastries and drinking hot coffee, and now the bargaining began. Pete knew everyone, and much of the negotiating was conducted in Italian. All around us were beautiful, glistening fruits and vegetables heaped in Rabelaisian profusion: zucchini, grapes, bunches of carrots, green, red and yellow peppers, cantaloupes and watermelons, and radicchio, fennel, green onions, leeks and Belgian endive, and firm green heads of lettuce and cabbage. The men shouted at each other in Italian. It seemed a little scary at first, but Pete assured me that this was just their way of making a deal.

Like lightning, the business would be concluded and soon Pete and I were loading the produce in the trailer. Pete would pull a gangster's roll of bills out of his pocket and pay up with 100's and 50's, and then the men would shake hands. Now they all seemed to be the very best of friends. Sometimes one of them would notice me and say something like, "So, you brought your helper along with you today, huh, Pete?"

By now it would be mid-morning and Pete and I were famished. Pete would back our trailer up against a brick wall and we'd take a taxi back to Little Italy. Usually we'd stop at Zampieri Brothers Bakery on Sullivan Street and buy hot, fresh loaves of Italian bread. To this we'd add some cheese and salami, plus fruit from our produce— grapes, plums, strawberries—and we'd go to nearby Washington Square Park, where we'd sit on a bench and stuff ourselves. Sometimes we'd go to Vincent's Clam Bar or to the White Horse Tavern, which opened at 11:00 on Sundays, the famous restaurant at 567 Hudson Street where Dylan Thomas drank himself to death in 1953.

Whenever we'd pass Saint Anthony's Cathedral at the corner of Houston and Sullivan, Pete would cross himself. Sometimes we'd stop and he'd go to Mass. I went inside once. It was dark and it smelled of incense, and there were icons, mysterious, holy-like. Ever since that day, Saint Anthony's, with its immense rose window, has remained in my mind as a symbol of New York and of Little Italy in particular.

When we got back to Cooperstown, how small everything seemed! Sometimes, as a special treat, Pete would drive down Pioneer Street and lean on the air horn, and I'd wave out the window of the Freightliner at Turk Monahan or Billy Stamford, or any of the Pioneer Street kids who happened to be out in front of their houses popping tar bubbles or riding bikes. We'd pass Mrs. Gio's Frog Hollow Grocery Market and maybe there'd be some kids coming out of the store with Popsicles, and Pete would blow the air horn again and I'd wave. At the top of Logan's Hill we'd make a right turn onto Church Street, then a left down into the little park by the Alfred Corning Clark Gymnasium and past the giant bronze JFC statue.

After Pete had parked our rig behind Guido's Market and we got everything unloaded, Pete and I had the task of trimming the vegetables and getting them ready to show. Pete chopped up the vegetables, I mean, he cleaned them, so quickly—washing, cutting, trimming—all the while breathing noisily through his hairy nostrils, as if his mouth were sealed, and sweating, sweating. Pete was a master with a French knife. That knife fairly flew. Outer leaves of lettuce, celery leaves, cabbage stalks, carrot trimmings— this excess greenery sailed through the air and littered the floor. I helped as best I could but I couldn't begin to keep up with Pete. Pete was a consummate produce man, a real artist.

Then we'd put everything out on display. Pete showed me how to arrange the celery and the endive and the asparagus. *Beautiful.* I know I must have been a pain in the ass. He had to tell me everything. Pete was middle-aged, with grown children. He must have been tired of kids. Still, he patiently explained everything to me.

At this juncture Pete, drenched with sweat but still smelling faintly of Bay Rum, would frequently pause and pop open a Genesee beer. Sometimes my father would drop by to have a few beers with Pete and talk about golf, and Pete would remark that "Young Rufus here" was a big help to him. Frequently tough-talking Carlo Capelleti, another of my father's golfing pals, would stop in for a drink. The Capelleti family owned a textile factory and some said a brothel in Utica. Later on, in the afternoon, if they weren't on the golf course, they'd all be playing a game of horseshoes in Pete's yard on Fair Street, or maybe attending a clambake at Three Mile Point or Fairy Springs.

Vinnie Martin came by too. He wasn't a golfer, but he

and Pete would talk Italian and drink an anisette. And on one memorable Sunday afternoon, I was confronted with the wonder and terror of the ragman's tigress of a daughter, the beautiful Marcie Martin, when she stopped in with her father. I was too shy even to say hello to her. Her perfume was heavenly, and I died a thousand deaths as I stood there stupidly chopping the vegetables.

3

After the Fairbanks haul and a peaceful but all-too-brief respite in LA, I hooked up with my old pal Roddy Joplin and we started running together out of Eureka.

Roddy Joplin was one of the haunted ones. Even though he'd recently married again, for the fifth time, and had financed a new tractor—every truck driver's dream—I knew, as Roddy himself must have known even then, that he'd never be able to lead a normal life. Roddy was hexed up, twisted, born under a bad star. In other words, Roddy had what it takes to be a writer.

I'd read some of Roddy's novel, *The Bridge*, but strangely enough I wasn't impressed. It was as though Hemingway had done a poor imitation of Faulkner with Steinbeck and John Dos Passos peering over his shoulder, and then F. Scott Fitzgerald had touched the thing up.

Roddy Joplin was a bona fide latter-day cowboy. As reckless as Roddy was about most things, he was meticulous when it came to his image. He wore embroidered western shirts, a three hundred-dollar alligator belt with an engraved silver ranger buckle and a Stetson Powder River buffalo hat that had set him back a hundred fifty smackers. And those Tony Lama reptile boots of his must have cost a small fortune. With his craggy face and brooding gaze, Roddy Joplin looked like a man who'd spent half his life branding longhorns on the Chisholm Trail.

All the way through Arizona and New Mexico, in the old days, when we ran together, we'd stop at every western clothing outlet and spend hours browsing while Roddy searched for a new belt buckle or for that special cowboy shirt. And whenever we'd park at a truck stop he'd carefully wipe his boots off with a red bandana before getting down from the cab. Roddy was a huge hit with the truck stop waitresses and with the girls in the cantinas, and even though I felt like a poor relation I was happy to ride along on his coattails. For me, it was like traveling with a celebrity.

Roddy's first marriage had ended in disaster when his young wife, Jolene, ran off with a chicken hauler from Rapid City, and two and three marriages later he was still carrying a torch for her. Add the Country & Western music and the beer and that was Roddy Joplin, the original iron-assed loser with a ten-gallon hat and a broken heart.

Roddy also had a keen intellect and an encyclopedic knowledge of world literature, but he never trotted this side of himself out, except with me, in the cab, when we were running miles or when we were quietly hashing things over at a bar or in a cantina somewhere. He had a slim, tattered volume, "Twenty-Five Poems," by Dylan Thomas, that he carried with him everywhere, from coast to coast. That book of Dylan Thomas poems was Roddy's Bible.

Whenever you ran with Roddy Joplin you'd better be ready to dance with the Devil. Roddy had a chip on his shoulder; he reveled in being an outsider. On our first trip out of Eureka we pulled a load of computer monitors down to El Paso and Roddy recited "And Death Shall Have No Dominion" by Dylan Thomas at the Crow Flite Truck Stop near Big Spring, Texas.

It had been a blazing hot day and we'd worked up a powerful thirst, so we stopped for beers at a roadhouse called Big Peckers. They had a huge statue of a chicken on the roof. We got pretty looped, especially Roddy, as usual. He was spoiling for a fight, and we nearly got into it with three JB Hunt drivers. I had to drag him out. I was scared, I admit it. Those JB Hunt guys were tough hombres and I didn't fancy tangling ass with them.

After Big Peckers we moseyed over to the Crow Flite, and Roddy brought along "Twenty-Five Poems" by Dylan Thomas. The Crow Flite was packed with truck drivers and field hands, real razorbacks, some of them big sunburned farm boys, and pretty soon in walks the three mouth-breathers from Big Peckers. "Well, this is it," I said to myself. But Roddy had other ideas. He ordered the bartender to turn the jukebox off, and then he climbed up on a table, opened the tattered poetry volume and began reading aloud. Roddy had great pipes, a rich baritone, as well as an appealing midwestern twang, and even though he was drunk, excellent diction.

> *"And death shall have no dominion.*
> *Dead men naked they shall be one*
> *With the man in the wind and the west moon..."*

Roddy read the whole thing, all three stanzas, then closed the book. A hush had fallen, like filtered moonlight descending on the prairie, and the room seemed dimmer somehow, and the faces of the men—blank, twitching, scrubbed clean of comprehension—were rag doll faces with polka-dot eyes and cross-stitched mouths. They were flabbergasted, utterly dumbfounded.

Roddy gazed defiantly around the silent room. "Anybody wanna say anything about that?"

There were no takers.

You always hear them say in the truck stops that if you miss a gear going down Donner Pass, you die. On our second trip out of Eureka I got a chance to find out if that was true. We had a load of cantaloupes for Pittsburgh.

Roddy was driving and I was in the jump seat. We pulled the long grade up Donner, parked in the brake inspection area near the sign, "Donner Summit—Elevation 7,239," and walked around the rig kicking the tires. After a little palaver about one thing and another we checked our brakes, and then we got ready to roll down toward Reno, with Roddy at the wheel.

Roddy selected a gear and we started down, but somehow he wound up in neutral. The rig was picking up speed. Roddy glanced quickly at me, then fumbled with the gearshift. He seemed to be doing everything in slow motion.

"Jesus Christ!"

The road was rushing up to meet us. Roddy gave me a challenging look: *What's the matter, can't you take it?*

We were now freewheeling down Donner Pass. Roddy seemed to be enjoying the danger, as well as my discomfort, and I strongly suspected that Roddy had missed that gear on purpose in order to scare the shit out of me in retribution for some the critical remarks I'd made about his novel.

We zoomed past another rig that seemed to be standing still, then swerved to avoid an approaching driver who leaned on his air horn. It was eerie, because even if he hadn't missed that gear on purpose, Roddy Joplin was the sort of desperado who didn't give a damn whether he lived or died. But I have to say that Roddy reacted perfectly once he'd made up his mind to do something. He stabbed the service brake several times, reducing our road speed, then tacked us up, lightly, gingerly, with just a toe-tap, and deftly grabbed a gear. The engine roared as the transmission engaged, and our rig, now under control, settled in behind another rig, and we continued our descent at safe speed.

The whole thing consumed less than two minutes, and neither one of us said a word about it. I did manage, however, a few hours later as we changed drivers at a truck stop, to say a couple of nice things about Roddy's manuscript, even though I didn't mean them.

Roddy's best work, in my opinion, was poured out in his long literary letters to me. It may well have been that Roddy was more of an essayist than a novelist. One of his favorite topics was the process by which certain individuals are factored out of the human equation and how this ordeal may lead, quite unexpectedly, to an extraordinary kind of freedom.

He'd broken the scenario down into four stages: *alienation, dehumanization, deracination* and *depersonalization*—a sort of Outsider's Personal Progress Index—with alienation as a starting point.

Alienation was a sort of social unease, a sense of not fitting in, a sense that one doesn't belong. Despite the volumes that have been written about it, alienation, Roddy insisted, is merely a preliminary phase, the shallowest of shallow waters, a baptism, so to speak.

After alienation comes dehumanization, which may be thought of as a postgraduate course on the heels of alienation. One's outsider identity is nicely confirmed. One has attained the status of social outcast, pariah, untouchable.

The next stage is deracination. Nationality and ethnicity drop away, like the discarded skin of a snake. One is no longer an American, a Frenchman, a Brit, a German, a Pole, a Jew. One is a displaced person, but still a person.

The final stage is depersonalization. One's failure as a human being is manifest. Name, rank, serial number, age, sex, height—all this becomes meaningless. You've been neatly factored out of the human equation. You're no longer a person. You simply *are.*

It's not that one has chosen to be cut out from the herd. It simply happens, to certain individuals. The process is painful and not at all voluntary. It's very much like childbirth in that respect.

What emerges, ultimately, is a primal entity,

untrammeled, anonymous, free. The layers of acquired detritus have been chipped away, the patina, the false cultural identity, the surface veneer that passes for being.

On our third trip out of Eureka we pulled forty thousand pounds of electronics to Buffalo, then ran up to Vermont to visit my Aunt Mizpah, but unfortunately she'd gone to Lake Dunmore for a few days so we ran over to Amherst to see the Emily Dickinson House.

As Roddy and I stood in the austere whitewashed bedroom where the Queen of Compressed Brilliance conducted her raids on the inarticulate, I could almost see Emily—"Saint Emily"—leaning out her window, lowering a basket of freshly baked gingerbread to the children below on the lawn.

Roddy read one of the poems aloud in Emily's garden. "A little Madness in the Spring."

A little Madness in the Spring
Is wholesome even for the King
But God be with the Clown —
Who ponders this tremendous scene —
This whole Experiment of Green —
As if it were his own!

Roddy had to get back to Clear Lake to see the missus so he dropped me off in New York. He was sorry we'd missed Aunt Mizpah, and I was sorry too, because I'd been looking forward to getting my two long-time literary correspondents together, but the visit to the Emily Dickinson House had been like visiting a shrine and both Roddy and I were keen now on getting some writing done. Over a final drink at the Angels Camp Tavern, a cellar bar on Houston near St. Anthony's Cathedral, we agreed that we no longer knew if we were running after something or running from something, but as Roddy declared, after tossing off a double shot of Bushmills,"The important thing is to run."

4

New York is a lonely town, but the Angels Camp Tavern was a friendly place. My roommates, Hal Feldman and Doyle Junghammer were fixtures, as was Parsifal the Poet, a pale, threadbare waif who traded poems scrawled on lavender-tinted paper to tourists for drinks. Most nights Tequila Lil (good smile, bad teeth) would be sitting at the bar with her sidekick, poor little Raggedy Ann, who peddled flowers in a Hebrew cemetery in Spanish Harlem. But it was blonde, halfway pretty Brenda Boudreau who caught my eye. Brenda kept to herself. Nobody at Angels Camp knew much about her except that she had a yellow cat named Taffy and her favorite drink was a vodka martini with three olives.

I spent most of my nights at Angels Camp huddled in a booth writing long literary letters to Roddy Joplin and Aunt Mizpah. Aunt Mizpah was considered odd by the family, and possibly even a little buggy, like Uncle Augustus and Grandma Maddalyn and my mother. And then of course there was the drinking. But I always thought maybe my mother was jealous of Aunt Mizpah because Aunt Mizpah inherited the old house at 61 Park Street in Brandon, the home of Judge John S. Niedenthal, the house in which Aunt Mizpah and my mother were raised after being orphaned by Grandma Maddalyn's suicide. And in later years, after Aunt Mizpah had settled down to the life of a proper New England spinster, and she and I began to correspond extensively, I even imagined that Aunt Mizpah had a secret cache of poems hidden away under the floorboards of the Judge's gloomy study, like the Comstock Lode of Emily Dickinson's poetry discovered after Emily's death by her younger sister Lavinia.

Actually, a huge cache was discovered at 61 Park Street in Brandon, according to Aunt Mizpah, some years back, before the Judge passed away and right after the death of Uncle Augustus, but it was a cache not of poems but rather a regular treasure trove of Uncle Augustus's erotic paper dolls, meticulously drawn, cut out and dressed by the eccentric old gentleman with the toenail scissors and the Homburg hat. The Judge ordered the "pornographic paper dolls" to be destroyed and so—quicker than a Brandon girl can eat blackberries—a valuable collection of art brut was lost to the world.

"You know, Jerzy, I think I'm getting closer to writing."

This announcement Hal Feldman made one afternoon at the Angels Camp Tavern, perched on his stool, elbows on the bar, resting his chin in his hand while sweeping the room with a benevolent gaze—as if marking this as a banner day that would live forever in our memories, the day on which Hal Feldman, our in-house celebrated writer, declared that in the not-too-distant future he might actually get around to *writing* something.

Hal had a way of talking about his novel, *Miss Nightingale's Dowry*, as if it actually existed, as if the galleys had just come back from the publisher and he was busy marking them up. And not only his novel in progress, *Miss Nightingale's Dowry*, but he somehow managed to give his listeners the impression that he'd already produced a considerable volume of work, a substantial *oeuvre*, in fact.

Hal was outrageously, impossibly, absurdly, unbearably handsome. His fire-glint eyes, black as olives, blazed dangerously behind a careless cascade of sensational curls. The girls at the bar were gaga over Hal, absolutely mesmerized by the flat-out magnetism of his bad boy looks, by the Presley pout of his lips as he filled the air with his buzzing swarms of magical winged words.

Sure, I envied Hal—glib, charming, facile, talking his book away in the bars as if he were pissing out a window. It was the brouhaha that spewed out of his mouth, that bright pissing stream of word magic that enabled Hal to live the writer's life *I* longed to lead. Hal was the writer I wanted to be—except for one thing. Hal was a writer who didn't write. His typewriter was in the pawnshop, in fact, and had been since I'd known him. It was Hal who complained about my typing, in the dismal spider's lair we shared at 67 Sullivan Street.

"Every time I talk, you start typing! Why is that?"

You don't get it, do you Hal? You just don't get it! I'm writing down everything you say, everything you do. You're my character, Boyo! Hop, you monkey! Do something amusing, for Christ's sake! You don't get it yet, do you? Hal, my lad, you're a bad lot, but you'll have to do.

Hal's unspoken motto, vis-à-vis the writing, was: bark loud enough and you'll never have to bite. And he didn't. Not a line. Not a trickle. Not a drop. Instead he managed a complete waste of words, day after day, night after night, at the bar, that fabulous brouhaha that spewed from his mouth and evaporated into thin air, like piss poured out of a boot.

Miss Nightingale's Dowry was one nervous nightingale, I can tell you. A bird on the wing, a regular Hindenburg Disaster. She was a high flier, that one. She flatly refused to come in for a landing, this fine-feathered friend of Hal's. She straggled along on a wing and a prayer, running on empty, her fuel gauges spinning like cuckoo clocks. *This way? That way?* What to do? She hovered over LaGuardia, feathering her props.

As for the dowry, not a penny in it. Hal's word-bank was bankrupt. You could smack it with a hammer and not even a pinfeather would come floating out. Hal's cupboard was bare. Four and twenty blackbirds? *I wouldn't count on it!* Words and words, pissed away like pennies into the wind. Like birdseed, like birdshot. *Gone!* Yes! That should have been your title, Hal, my boy! *Gone With the Wind...*

My other roommate, Doyle Junghammer, an ex-football player who worked as a bouncer at a strip club, was also trying to be a writer. We lifted weights together in the apartment at 67 Sullivan. Doyle's idol was Hemingway. He saw himself as a soldier of fortune and even subscribed to *Soldier of Fortune Magazine.* He wanted to live the Hemingway lifestyle: the Côte d'Azur, the black Bugatti, the French fisherman shirts and linen trousers, the martinis with garlic olives—and the house in Key West, of course.

Doyle's dream was to build a house of his own in Key West—the "Tiki House" he called it. He'd already had the plans drawn up. It was a sort of private empire where he'd be able to do exactly as he pleased. To accomplish his dream of course he would need money, a lot of money. How would he get the money? Doyle's answer was by making a big score, while he was still young. His plan was to go to South America and bring back: gold, diamonds, emeralds, whatever the earth had to offer, and he wanted me to go along.

"If you want to be a writer," Doyle told me one night after I'd handed him his last set of bench presses, "there are three ways to do it. One, be born rich. Two, marry a rich woman. Three, strike it rich—early in life. That way you'll have the leisure to study, to research, to contemplate, to write. I know what's involved, believe me. I've looked into it. I'm not a 'dumb jock,' Jerzy, regardless of what people say. Does that surprise you? Listen to me: writing is a rich man's game. A writer without money is condemned to live in the streets."

Hal and I did some rough carpentry at the studio of pastiche artist Theo Pritikin, knocking together frames for stretching the burlap and muslin he used in his work. And some small jobs on Houston and Canal, drywall, painting, and a little plumbing. We built duckboards for the bar, Angels Camp Tavern, and also for the White Horse Tavern on Hudson Street made famous by Dylan Thomas. Neither of us knew much about plumbing or hanging sheetrock, but Hal had the tools, and ever the schmoozer, he found us plenty of jobs. But somehow—I don't know how to put it—the whole thing was shot in the ass. Neither of us was at all serious about life. Typically, we'd take our front money to the bar and get sloshed, then piss away our working hours talking about Hal's nonexistent book.

On my solitary walks through the city, from the Fulton Fish Market to the Battery, from Central Park to West 4th Street, I found myself forever peering in shop windows, not in the windows exactly, but at the surface of the glass, to see if my image was reflected there. Did I exist at all? Or was I a phantom, a wraith, a vapor, an apparition? Afraid I might blow away on a breeze, I longed for a pair of lead shoes. Smaller than a gnat, I was convinced of nothing if not my invisibility. For this reason the problem, for me, vis-à-vis the writing, never had to do with plot or character development, but rather the problem was, simply stated: *how can I make myself visible to others?*

Alienation, dehumanization, deracination, depersonalization. I was moving right along, according to the Outsider's Index. Of course I had a leg up, genetically speaking, with my mad Uncle Augustus who lived in a tree and all.

I spent hours writing on the subway walls with a magic marker. My favorite spot was the subway entrance at West 4th Street, right across from Barnes & Noble. I'd copy passages out of my novel-in-progress, then I'd lurk nearby and watch to see if I got any readers. One of my favorite tricks was to make derogatory remarks about my wall scribbling by way of eliciting comments from passersby, who, as often as not, would defend the work as having "redeeming social value," or better, "a certain lyric quality." Remarks like these sent me into raptures and spurred me on to write like a house afire.

One day the bartender at Angels Camp handed me a package from Aunt Mizpah. She'd sent it to the bar for some reason. Aunt Mizpah had unearthed a Civil War diary written by a Brandon cousin, John Sebastian Shimmersaltz, who enlisted in the Union Army in 1861, along with his two brothers, Tom and Wendell. The Shimmersaltz brothers fought with the Army of Western Tennessee under U.S. Grant. All three brothers were killed on April 6, 1862, at Shiloh, where the butcher's bill for the day was 23,746 killed, wounded, missing, Confederate and Union soldiers combined.

Also in the package was the Homer Laughlin Virginia Rose child's tea set that had belonged to Aunt Mizpah's twin sisters, Helga and Hulda, who were poisoned by their mother, Maddalyn Isolde Shimmersalz, my maternal grandmother, on that fateful summer morning after the Whippoorwill Farm fire when she drank the deadly Paris Green. The twins, Aunt Mizpah reported, loved to have tea parties with their dolls underneath the towering elms in the back yard, the tallest of which, Aunt Mizpah claimed, was felled by lightning on the day after the deaths. It was my mother, in fact, who discovered the bodies—her mother, Maddalyn, and the twins, Helga and Hulda. How peaceful they looked, underneath the elms, the tiny twin girls, with their little teacups still in their hands! How still they were. How cold to the touch. It may well be that my mother went off her nut right then and there, but Aunt Mizpah had confided to me in her letters that my mother, Ellen Smeisser Shimmersalz, had been from earliest childhood, well before the fire, a dour and cheerless individual.

But the teacups, Helga and Hulda's ornate, delicate little teacups… Why Aunt Mizpah sent those precious teacups to me for safekeeping—me, the black sheep of the family—I'll never know. The logical person would have been my sister Erin, who lived a sedate and normal life, and I resolved to get them to her as soon as possible for safekeeping.

I didn't like being Hal's sidekick, and besides it was all dreary, empty, futile. I mean the scruffy slapdash lifestyle, the beery, bloated conversations at the bar and stumbling through the days in an alcoholic fog. And for what? Chump change! Weeks went by like that, months. Sometimes when I was halfway sober I'd go into St. Anthony's Cathedral, corner of Sullivan and Houston, and sit there like I was praying. Nobody seemed to notice me. One day when I stepped outside I heard some kids singing, *"St. Anthony, St. Anthony, please come down. Something is lost and must be found."* I knew that something was me. I had a sickening sense that life was passing me by. I should have been going home every night to a wife, two children and a yard full of pink plastic lawn flamingoes. I was sinking deeper and deeper into the muck. I was high on despair. I had to get out of New York.

I figured I had two options: I could go back on the road for Mercury Movers, or I could go to Iowa and join Roddy Joplin who was running once again out of Clear Lake, and maybe make some real money. But while I was trying to decide between the frying pan and the fire I got a call from Reggie Ray. Armando was back, his co-driver had bailed on him and he was on his way to NYC with a load for Astoria Heights. After which he'd be picking up thirty thousand pounds for Charleston, Macon, Jeanerette, Port St. Joe, Palmetto and Miami, and *could I possibly..?* Like an idiot I said yes.

Just before I left Parsifal the Poet was killed, right in

front of the Angels Camp Tavern, hit by a car. The meat wagon had already carted him away when I arrived. It was nobody's fault, I learned. The car had skidded and jumped the curb in the blinding rain. Tequila Lil and Raggedy Ann were standing outside the bar, in tears, and some of Parsifal's rain-soaked lavender poems were scattered in the gutter. Brenda Boudreau emerged from the bar, hugging her yellow cat, Taffy. I picked up one of Parsifal's poems—I don't know why—and handed it to Brenda. "Maybe we could dry them out," she murmured with a hopeless smile. The rain was coming down hard, and the cat, drenched, set up a demented yowling.

The trip with Armando went swimmingly at first—at least my winged feet were getting me out of New York—but then after we unloaded in Miami we went to a bar in Little Havana and there was Conchita, Conchita from Cienfuegos, and she and Armando hit it off right away. Conchita was dying to get to California and three's a crowd, so I grabbed my old blue canvas gym bag and—hey, let's give the Sunshine State a whirl. Why not leave one's destiny entirely to chance and simply surrender to the flow of life? It seemed to me that everything I'd tried to do had pretty much ended up in the toilet. Maybe I should take my hands off the wheel and give up even the pretense of steering. This moment and this moment and this moment. Why connect the dots? But I was sorry to leave Armando. We were getting to be great pals.

.

5

Big Bill Sturdyvant was the booziest bastard I ever met. The former mercenary soldier and owner of the Piñacolada Bar on NE 54th Street in Miami engaged me to ghostwrite his autobiography. Bill Sturdyvant was a real-life Hemingway hero, an older Doyle Junghammer. We'd meet in his office at the bar. He wore a raw silk shirt, an officer's dress cap, and he was forever clamping a dead cigar. I'd show him my pages and he'd peel a few bills off his roll. Usually, he was pleased with my work, and of course this called for a drink. One drink led to another, and pretty soon he'd lean back in his swivel chair, squint at me over his whiskey and soda, and ask, "Ever eat monkey?" And no matter whether I answered yes or no, we were off, tramping through the Bolivian jungle packing pump action shotguns and KA-BAR combat knives.

The Piñacolada, Big Bill's bar, was full of war souvenirs, especially Flying Tigers memorabilia. There was a parrot, too, in a wrought iron cage at the end of the bar. On the wall in the office was a photo of Big Bill training counter terrorist forces in Nicaragua, and one of Lúcio Flávio, the famous Brazillian bandit who was killed by a death squad in 1975.

I was happy. I was off the road and I had myself a meal

ticket. I cranked out my pages and got my advances. It was a pretty sweet deal. I didn't like the war stories and I didn't like drinking so much, especially whiskey, so when Big Bill wasn't looking I'd pour some of my drink into the potted plant on his desk. After a month that plant died, probably of alcohol poisoning. I would have preferred wine, but I didn't want to bring that up either. Big bill would almost certainly have thought I was a sissy. He was a man's man—the whiskey voice, the cigar smoke, the straight from the shoulder palaver, and all that. He had a cut glass decanter, like the ones you see in the 40's movies. He seemed to live entirely in the past.

I had to drive him places, too, in his '57 DeSoto. He was usually as potted as his plant.

Mariska was the barmaid at the Piñacolada. She was also "Lady Mariska," a popular dominatrix. Lady Mariska was pretty enough, but she had a good ten years on me. Still, she turned me on. She frequently wore a black lycra cat suit to work. The bird was hers, Cap'n Ike, the parrot. The parrot talked a lot, but he spoke only Hungarian, except for two phrases, "*Kommen Sie hier, Liebling*," and "Worship my feets!" Lady Mariska insisted that the bird's real name was László, for her father, who talked a blue streak, but Big Bill had renamed him Cap'n Ike, and the name stuck. Lady Mariska had a dog, too, a pug, a walleyed little bugger named Otto.

Przybyszewski, a retired master sergeant, was a regular at the bar. He was one of Lady Mariska's clients. This Przybyszewski used to take me to a dim sum restaurant, where he'd insist on ordering for me. *Char siu bao*, sesame seed balls, spareribs, *shu mai*, spring rolls; it all came at once, the food, and half of it was cold before you could eat it. It pissed me off but he was buying so I didn't say anything. He was a decent guy, Przybyszewski, but he was still a master sergeant in his heart and would always be one, so once I got back into the Army way of doing things we got along fine.

Hymen Przybyszewski's gentile name was Harry. "Hymen" was reserved for his family and his Jewish friends. Przybyszewski's gentile friends called him "Top," for Top Sergeant, and that's what I called him.

Top had dozens of pairs of women's shoes, mostly stiletto heels, in his huge walk-in closet. His dress uniform with master sergeant's stripes—three up and three down—was hanging there too, and the jacket was one big fruit salad: Purple Heart, airborne wings, Combat Infantryman, the Silver Star, the Bronze Star and plenty more. Unlike Big Bill, Top never talked much about the war. He'd been through Korea and half of Vietnam on the ground, an infantry soldier. Top had been wounded during the Tet Offensive, but he never said anything more about it than that.

When things were slow at the bar, Lady Mariska used to tell me stories about Top. "Yesterday my little Przybyszewski invited me to drink a cocktail with him. He could not resist my sexy ass and he worshipped my stilettos. *Worship my feets*, I tell him. *Worship my feets!* It is very hot for me to see this little Przybyszewski worship my feets."

The main thing we did, Top and I, besides drink at the bar and eat dim sum, was make horseradish sauce together. First we'd go to the supermarket and buy the horseradish roots. They had to be firm, not rubbery, with dark green leaves. Back at the apartment we'd scrub the horseradish roots with a vegetable brush. Top insisted that we wear rubber gloves. I was allowed to help peel the horseradish roots, but he'd never let me do anything further except listen while he talked about his childhood in Brooklyn. He'd cut the roots up in small pieces and run them through a blender. You had to stand clear when he took the lid off the blender. Top's horseradish sauce was potent. The kitchen windows had to be open and he'd even jokingly suggest that we wear gasmasks. Toward the end of the procedure he'd add half a cup of vinegar, which he said locked in the heat, and finally, to cool the stuff down a bit and add a deep red color, he'd pour in some beet juice.

Top realized that I was a *luftmensh*, meaning a dreamer who has trouble making a living.

"*Vermicomposting*," he said to me one day. "Vermicomposting. That's the ticket for you, Boychick. It's a piece of cake."

Vermicomposting. He wanted me to start a worm farm. He meant well, I'm sure of that.

"I've looked into it. Worms are simple creatures. They eat, they fuck and they shit. You sell the castings for fertilizer and the worms for bait. They're high in nitrogen, the castings. Sound like a pretty good deal? You use red worms, red wrigglers, they're called, not night crawlers. A worm eats half his body weight each day. They eat garbage, so you get rid of your garbage. You'll have plenty of time to write, believe me."

Top meant well, as I say, he had my best interests at heart, but he was used to commanding men. He didn't want to hear the word "no". Myself, I just couldn't see it, wading around knee deep in worms all day. How could I ever eat spaghetti again? I didn't want to accept the mission but didn't know how to squirm out of it. I was about to call Roddy Joplin, but then I got a letter from Roddy postmarked Nuevo Laredo. Roddy had become obsessed with the idea that he might have a child in a Mexican whorehouse somewhere, and on this account he'd left his fifth marriage and had embarked on a tour of the Mexican brothels from Matamoros to Tijuana searching for his mythical kid. Same old Roddy!

Leon Pheiffer reminded me of a man roller-skating through chicken shit. He sailed along beautifully, but somehow he managed at every moment to spatter himself with ordure. The man radiated a peculiar combination of insouciance and desperation. With Leon, the disadvantages gained always seemed to outweigh the advantages incurred.

He was his own best enemy, you might say.

I met Leon Pheiffer at the Piñacolada, or rather, just outside the Piñacolada, in the street. He hit me up for spare change. We talked briefly, then I invited him into the bar for a sandwich and a glass of beer. After a second beer he showed me some of his poems. I was impressed. When, after a few more brews, I learned just how desperate his circumstances were, I invited him home with me. That was a mistake. From that moment forward, Leon Pheiffer stuck to me like a leech.

His poetry, so he said, had been published in some of the literary journals. Undoubtedly, he could have published a great deal more, but the bulk of his work was scrawled on napkins and scraps of brown bag paper. He had no typewriter. There was no order in his life. He'd recently hitchhiked from New York to Miami. He didn't know why. He mentioned a manuscript that he'd carried with him, the result of two years labor. He'd left it in a bus station locker in Charleston, he thought. Or maybe it was Richmond.

Only in his middle twenties, he'd already been fired from more than fifty jobs. Leon Pheiffer was tall, strong, extremely healthy, keenly intelligent, marvelously articulate and completely unemployable. He had only one desire—to go on with his writing regardless of the consequences. Actually, he had no choice but to write. When fits of "dictation" came over him, as they frequently did, in restaurants, for example, or at the bar, he'd scribble on the tablecloth or the menu or on any scrap of paper he could find. In these moments, when his eyes were fixed on some invisible drama and his face reflected a parade of passing emotions, there was something of the oracle about him. Leon Pheiffer was a seer, a prophet, the avatar of his own imagination.

Just the same, life with Leon was terribly difficult. I was subsisting on my income from Big Bill's autobiography. Now, with two mouths to feed, I was using up my advances far too quickly and falling behind on my deadlines. I couldn't type because Leon talked incessantly. He never left my side, not even for a moment. His need to talk was obsessive. Frequently, after these all-day and all-night talk sessions, I felt as if I'd been battered with a pugil stick. The only respite I had from his constant chattering was when I went to the toilet, or he did. Often there was no money in the house and we got by on such small sums as I managed to borrow from Top or Lady Mariska. Leon ate like a horse, yet he never volunteered to fix a meal, never washed a dish and never took out the trash. At night, it took him hours to settle down. His one desire was to talk, to spill it out, and my only thought was to wrap the pillow around my head and go to sleep, to shut him off, to silence him and stuff his mouth with eiderdown. Leon was bursting with energy and enthusiasm, but—how to explain it—there was nothing in that multi-leveled, multi-faceted activity of his that was directed toward practical ends.

One morning, in order to give him a hint, I took him to a shape-up and got us a day's work loading moving vans at a warehouse in Hialeah. We picked up sixty bucks apiece, under the table, and that was super, but still Leon didn't get the idea. He immediately blew his earnings on champagne and lobster. Leon didn't know how to soldier, he didn't know how to scramble, and he wasn't interested in learning. He couldn't or wouldn't understand that he was becoming an intolerable burden, that he was driving me crazy. On my part I understood instinctively that I would have to cut this joker loose, and soon, or he would drag me down with him into the street, an eventuality that I was determined to avoid at any cost.

I told Lady Mariska about my problem and she put me in touch with the vice president of a bank, an old queen named Mr. Flebisher. This Flebisher was going to Paris soon and he was looking for a traveling companion. He was offering five hundred bucks plus expenses. Leon had talked a great deal about Paris. He'd often spoken about his poet friend Avril Ostander, who worked at the American Embassy. He'd frequently assured me that this Ostander would gladly take him in if somehow he could get across the pond. Suddenly it all fell together. I saw my chance—to get rid of Leon, and to give him a shot at a new life, on the other side of the world. For Leon, it was the opportunity of a lifetime. And for me it meant peace and quiet and time to get some writing done. *C'est magnifique!* We had a drink at the bar.

"America's no place for you," I prattled glibly. "Believe this: I'll be out of here myself, just as soon as I can manage it."

"You're right, Jerzy. You're so right!"

I thought Leon was going for it, hook, line and sinker, but when we got back to the room he began to get cold feet. Standing in front of the mirror, he picked up my toothpaste and squirted some on his finger and rubbed it around on his teeth, gently rocking from one foot to the other and humming the introduction to "LA Woman."

"You know," he muttered, "it was great of Mariska to look out for me like this. She's really a..."

"Yeah, I know. She's a prince of a woman."

Leon finished scrubbing his teeth and inspected them again in the cracked mirror. He announced that his teeth had a greenish tinge to them. Or maybe the mirror was dirty, he couldn't tell.

"I wonder what *his* teeth'll look like, Mr. Flebisher's?" he said suddenly. "Probably greenish too, or brownish..."

I switched off my typewriter and started rummaging around for change. I'd decided we were going back to the bar. Anything was better than this.

"I've got three dollars and something, three dollars and forty-nine—"

"*Christ!*" Leon exclaimed, clapping a hand over his eyes and flopping down suddenly on the bed, *my* bed. "My head feels like an anthill. Millions of goddamn thoughts crawling over each other, like insects. Ever have that? *The insect activity of the mind!* I can't get any relief. I can't stop thinking about him, the gay bastard, Mr. Flebisher."

Next day, same business; we had breakfast at the bar, on my tab.

"What are you thinking about?" Leon asked me as he picked at his scrambled eggs.

"About your trip to Paris, the flight, the stewardesses, the champagne, all that. A new life, brother! Jesus, it's going to be beautiful."

"Sure," he muttered, a little nonplused at my effusiveness. "You're right, as always, brother. Might as well look on the bright side of things."

"Sure."

"Christ, it's not going to kill me."

"Of course not."

Leon gazed at me hopelessly over his coffee cup. His face crumpled into a tortured frown. "I've got this feeling that his palms are going to be sweaty. Real sweaty. You know what I mean? And he'll have those short pudgy fingers that bankers have..."

Lady Mariska picked up our dishes. I looked over at Leon, bristling and sweating like a marble porcupine. If only I could have bolstered him, if only I could have injected a little pizzazz into him. But I kept forgetting that Leon was a masochist. His instincts were perverse. He loved to stew in his own juice. He poked himself with his own porcupine quills while huge beads of sweat popped out along the faint hairline crack in his magnificent marble forehead. That was ecstasy to him!

More beers. Leon is chewing his nails. His mind, as always, leaps ahead, supplying the details. Where the normal man might see one or two possibilities, Leon sees a hundred, two hundred possibilities. His mind is too agile. He knows what's going to happen, or so he thinks. He *thinks*, that's the problem.

Now he's talking about the room at the Hotel Sofitel Paris where the two of them will be holed up.

"It's near the Arc de Triomph, you know. It'll have oak paneling, or maybe mahogany, and they'll have those little mints on a silver tray. And everything'll smell fresh and clean... I once stayed in a place like that in North Carolina, when I was a kid. I'll never forget that trip. My stepbrother came and got me out of the orphanage. They had black dudes in uniforms at the motel. They brought you ice water on a tray. At night you could hear the frogs cheeping. And there was this smell, this wonderful piney smell. I felt so safe, and...so happy to be out of the joint. What the hell, Jerzy, you know, now that I think of it, it's not going to be so bad."

"Now you're talking. Look, don't think of it as an ordeal. Think of it as an opportunity."

"Sure. You're right. I know that." Leon nodded uncertainly. "I could turn up the air conditioner while he's asleep. That way he won't sweat so much."

It was becoming obvious to me that my scheme to get rid of Leon wasn't going to pan out. It worked fine on paper, as they say.

Then a lot of things happened, and I started getting pretty chummy with Lady Mariska. I'd drive her around in Big Bill's DeSoto. Top didn't care, of course, he was Lady Mariska's client, not her boyfriend, but Big Bill was pissed off. He'd take my pages and tear them up, tell me to start over. And he wouldn't pay me. I learned too that Lady Mariska had been knocking down, I mean at the cash register, and for a long time. She'd embezzled a couple grand, it turned out. And Top did warn me, in a friendly way, like a sergeant to a corporal, that I was getting in over my head.

"She's bad news, Boychick. It ain't just an act with her, you know, this domination business. She's a man hater. You'd be better off shtupping a rattlesnake."

Then M'Butu came to my door, M'Butu from Mogadishu. I couldn't believe it. Armando had been deported again and Reggie Ray wanted me to come back, so he sent M'Butu from Mogadishu. How Reggie Ray found me, I'll never know. He was a spider, Reggie Ray, an octopus with a million tentacles. M'Butu had a load for Key West. He'd pick me up on the back side, he said. One didn't say "no" to M'Butu from Mogadishu. You simply didn't. You didn't even say "maybe". I was plenty spooked.

Lucky for me, the very next day Lady Mariska asked me to drive her to the Sabal Palm Drugstore so she could get her Vicodin. Nothing unusual about that, except I noticed that she'd loaded a bunch of her belongings in the back. And after we'd picked up her prescription she told me to keep on driving north. She said she was going to move in with her sister in Fort Lauderdale. But when we got to Fort Lauderdale, I was the same thing. *"Keep driving, Liebling!"* Then I realized what was going down. She was running away from the Piñacolada, away from Big Bill— that is, *we* were running away, and we'd taken the DeSoto, and if he reported it and the cops caught up with us, I was looking at grand theft auto.

Why didn't I jump ship right then and leave Lady Mariska in the lurch? There was the sexual thing, but more than that I saw my chance to get away from Leon. If I couldn't send Leon to Paris, I could send myself to wherever it was that Lady Mariska and I were headed. The ghostwriting gig with Big Bill had completely fizzled thanks to my affair with Lady Mariska. I was two months behind on the rent and I wasn't leaving any possessions except my battered old Smith Corona. I hated to desert Top; Top was a hell of a nice guy, but he'd become so damned insistent about my starting the worm farm… The shit had pretty much hit the fan for me in Miami. Winged feet, do your stuff! It was time to cut a chogie.

Soon we were rolling through the Everglades in the DeSoto. In the back seat were Lady Mariska's belongings, hatboxes, wigs, stiletto heels, and her pug, Otto, a snappish, flea-infested little beast, plus the bird from the bar, Cap'n Ike, the parrot, in his cage.

Cap'n Ike was very much like Lady Mariska: shrewd, calculating, heartless. I watched him in the rear view mirror as I piloted the great ark. He reminded me of an old sea captain picking the lice out of his feathers. He kept honing his beak on the bars of the cage, with a greedy, savvy glitter in his eye. He'd cock his head from side to side, glaring at me, as though he were taking the measure of me and finding me not quite to his liking. At times, as I watched, he almost seemed to be puffing on a cigar and strutting up and down like an arrogant little gangster. He'd curse me in Hungarian, and then squawk, "*Kommen Sie hier, Liebling*," and "*Worship my feets!*" He was a dirty little devil, but all the same I couldn't help laughing at his comical antics.

Cap'n Ike was okay, but the damned pug was insufferable. He yipped and yapped and nipped at our flea-bitten ankles. He was a breeding farm for fleas, and so were Lady Mariska and I. Everything was infested. The fleas kept pinging up off the floor mats. It sometimes happened that I had my pants off and it felt like a light rain of buckshot was falling on my thighs. I despised that pug so whenever I got the chance, like when we stopped for a picnic, I tormented him. While pretending to be nice to him I'd pick him up like a football and hold him at arms length for an inordinate amount of time. He'd swivel his head frantically on his absurdly short neck, the walleyed little bugger, waving his runty legs like a damned horseshoe crab. There was never anyone quite so *ineffectual* as this little character.

At night the swamp was alive with frog cheeps and deep-bellied bullfrog burps. The air was thick and black. Powdery moths the size of sparrows dive-bombed our headlights. One night, when we stopped to sleep, I tied Otto's leash to the front bumper in hopes that a gator would eat him. In the morning the heat shimmered up off the pavement, a snowy egret gulped down a writhing snake, and a great green turtle plodded across the highway and disappeared into the saw grass.

Lady Mariska was a fraud. Her façade went clear through. She was one solid ingot of baked enamel. I never knew her, except in the Biblical sense. I might as well have been shagging a reindeer or a she-ass for all the communication there was between us. She was a hothouse flower, full-fledged and breathy, perpetually at full bloom. Her hair, piled up, twirled around and interwoven like a wicker basket, was sprayed stiff as a birdcage. And inside the birdcage a canary was chirping. While I drove she spent hours plucking her eyebrows, peering cannily into a tiny mirror with a queenly air of enormous confidence, as if in her mind she were planning some grand venture. Which of course she was. She lived almost entirely in the future.

Lady Mariska had a carnival-flair and a ballyhoo she could lay down without really trying. It was no act with her. I was amused at first by all this, the hype, the shell game, but she couldn't shut it off, and before long it began to wear thin with me. As we rolled through the Everglades we stopped at one Stukey's after another, as well as at every alligator farm and monkey jungle. Lady Mariska had to con everybody we met, or at the very least she had to assure herself that she could con them, that she held them in the palm of her hand. Then we were free to move on.

"We will stop for the gas in Okaloosa. I must call New York. I think Vadim has some papers for me to sign. Did you know I sold my life story to Viking? The first half only, to age 27. And do not forget to check the oil when we get to Akapoola. You know where the dipstick is, don't you, *Leibling?*"

The sky was scrubbed clean of clouds as we emerged at last from the glades on the heels of a towering thunderstorm, and barefoot kids were selling chinquapins by the side of the road. Near New Iberia we stayed over at Belle Isle, an antebellum plantation house built in 1831, where I met the famous sculptor Bronco Childress, who had recently draped hundreds of roadside trees across Louisiana with miles of glittery gauze-like ribbons.

Bronco was a wild man, a human impact wrench. His blond dreadlocks fanned out peacock-like from the top of his skull. We took a stroll through the Peach Orchard to a spot near the Manneken Pis fountain—a replica of the celebrated "Peeing Boy" statue that stands near the Grande Place in Brussels—where Bronco was building a concrete boat. He was planning to sail to Belize. You wouldn't think a concrete boat would float, but Bronco said it would. He'd been adding vermiculite, perlite and crushed corncobs to the mix to make the concrete lighter.

"It's a matter of density," he explained.

Mariska and I slept that night in a four-poster canopied bed. On the wall above the fireplace was a haunting portrait of a slave entitled, "Mathilda, Creole Negress," painted in 1851, a girl so beautiful she could have made the movies hands down if she'd been born in the twentieth century.

On the day we left I watched Bronco come vaulting out of the Peach Orchard with a rebar bender in his hand, his crazy dreadlocks popping out from under a Swiss mountaineer's hat. He hopped gingerly on top of his half-finished concrete boat and stood there, shirtless, his segmented torso gleaming with sweat, bristling with sinister tattoos. Preening and strutting, all Gypsy-like insouciance and devil-may-care bravado, he was snapping his fingers in time with some inaudible tune. Bronco's secret—the secret of his charisma, of his joie de vivre— was that he loved being Bronco. He adored being Bronco. He celebrated his Bronco-ness, he shouted it from the rooftops. Most people, I've observed, don't particularly like the roles they've been assigned by central casting. Bronco Childress was different. He was thrilled to be playing Bronco. Every day was a new adventure for him. Bronco was having great fun simply being Bronco. That was his secret.

Kommen Sie hier, Liebling! What an idiot I was. Top was right. Lady Mariska didn't give a rat's ass about me. When we got over to New Orleans she found a handsome young tour guide named Pierre Lejeune to drive the car and shtup her off, and she left me in the soup.

After I got settled in New Orleans, Land of Dreams, at a homey little place called the Palais Royale, I sent Top a postcard and said I was sorry about the worm farm. Several months after that he informed me in a letter that Big Bill had finally managed to drink himself to death and that the Piñacolada was closed. Top was kind enough to send my typewriter to me, too, via FedEx, the old pink Smith Corona I'd left behind when Lady Mariska and I flew the coop. And he invited me to move in with him, rent-free. Top was lonely, I knew, and it was a tempting offer—I was busting suds at a restaurant in the French Quarter—but for some reason I didn't go. I did run into Leon Pfeiffer again, however, a year later in Paris. But that's another story.

6

I was in love with Diamanta Real. That was my misfortune. I thought of myself as her significant other, but as things progressed I learned that I was merely one of several significant others and that I was not nearly as significant as some of the other significant others.

Diamanta had two wolfhounds, Saluki and WindSurfer. Like her, they were aristocratic, cool, remote. We walked them every evening in the hills behind the avocado grove at the house in Bonsall—or "Bons'll," as the locals say— about a hundred miles south of LA on Highway #76. Diamanta was house sitting while her mother was in Spain. The place was an elegant multi-level Italian villa with five bedrooms, a formal dining room, three fireplaces, a pebble-bottom spa, a gazebo and an avocado grove. We called it "the Castle". It was Diamanta who told me that wolfhounds should not be allowed to run loose, because once they begin to run, there's a very good chance that they won't come back.

Diamanta was quite up front about Bruno, the disbarred dentist from Santa Barbara. Just before we met she'd gone down to Mexico City to visit him. Bruno had a criminal record and lived most of the time in Venezuela, which has no extradition treaty with the United States.

He'd driven his Porsche from Caracas to Mexico City for the tryst with Diamanta.

Diamanta was more secretive about Gary and Daryl. Gary was a fellow drug counselor at the Scripps MacDonald Center in La Jolla where Diamanta worked, and Daryl was a computer programmer who emailed her spicy photos from Internet porn sites. Sigurd was much younger, a professional snowboarder from Iceland. Scott was younger, too, a personal trainer who worked at Gold's Gym. Well, do I need to go on?

Gary and Daryl and I occupied about the same status. We were entertainments only and our suits for Diamanta's hand weren't taken seriously. Bruno was in another class entirely. Bruno was the Alpha Male. Women claim that they want a man who is sensitive, considerate and romantic, but this is pure bullshit. Invariably, they give their hearts to the Alpha Male who rides his motorcycle into the living room, flops down on the couch and snarls, *"Fix me sompin' da eat, bitch!"*

Diamanta Real's family was Spanish, not Mexican. She made that crystal clear from the start. She claimed she came from a long line of Spanish Grandees. And it's certainly true—as I found out—that she did have what is called "a cold Spanish heart". She was cool, aloof, distant, except when she was drunk. The only time we made love was when she was pretty well liquored up. She was also cold in a physical sense. She said it was poor circulation. Even in the warmest weather she often wore a Russian sable fur coat, a full-length mink or a chinchilla jacket.

When I was a kid my Aunt Mizpah used to read to me, fairy tales. A big favorite of mine was "The Snow Queen" by Hans Christian Andersen. The Snow Queen lived in a castle made of ice. There was a magic mirror, and it broke and shattered into a million pieces, and a little orphan boy got a tiny splinter of glass in his eye and his vision was distorted. He couldn't see things the way they really were. The Snow Queen invited the little orphan boy into her ice palace, and I still remember the exact words from the story:

"Come into my arms," said the Snow Queen, opening her soft fur coat. "Come and keep warm."

Now I was that little boy with the splinter of glass in his eye. I couldn't see the truth about my Snow Queen, Diamanta Real. I didn't want to know the truth, so I only saw what I wanted to see.

Right after I met Diamanta I went back on the road. Not for Mercury Movers this time: I signed on with Schneider National. I was serious about Diamanta and, consequently, I decided to get serious about life. I knew, of course, what I was letting myself in for. Being a truck driver is just like being homeless, except you've got money to eat. You go down the road and it's interesting— *sometimes*. But it gets old, like after your one hundred seventeenth trip to Detroit. When you become a truck driver you meet up with all kinds of social desperadoes. Just about everybody out there has some sort of catastrophe behind him—divorce, bankruptcy, a lost business—so they go on the road. It's the Legion of Lost Souls, the Legion of the Damned. Sure, there's your upper crust of independent contractors with their fancy Peterbilt conventionals and their wives and their little dogs, but below that it's a mix of misfits and fuck-ups.

It's lonely as hell, all those miles. Most guys will run the radio or talk on the CB, anything but face their own emptiness. What it means is being disconnected from life except for the blacktop and that white line. You go into a truck stop and they've got signs reading *"Professional Drivers Only"* and you've got your phones at the tables, and for fifteen minutes you feel like somebody. Then you get back out there and it's just you and that white line. I'm not saying it's all bad. You pull into a truck stop and everybody's jungling up for the night—Werner, Swift, England, JB Hunt—and their engines are turning over, and you feel safe. There's a sense of community. Plus it's a great way to see the country. You take it in, the vastness of America, and you blow it all out your stacks.

After my piss test and whatnot I stuffed a few things in my gym bag, said goodbye to Diamanta and went up to the Operating Center in Montebello for ADT (Advanced Driver Training). It's three days in the classroom and four days driving locally with a trainer. Your lodging is paid and you're issued meal tickets and you're on a salary.

I passed my company road test and went on to the Skid Pad. You go down a hill at 50 mph and launch onto a concrete pad flooded with water. A trainer in the jump seat beside you locks your brakes electronically and puts you in a trailer jackknife. You have to declutch and steer out of it. Basically, you stay off the brakes and off the throttle. You steer in the direction of the skid, get your wheels lined up, then you get on the fuel. All this must be done automatically and very quickly. Like a great many things in life, it works a whole lot better if you don't think about it.

After the Skid Pad I went back to Bonsall to wait to be called back to Montebello for my road trip with a trainer. Diamanta met me at the door of the Castle wearing nothing but her Russian sable fur coat and her black elbow-length Lily Langtree opera gloves. I was overjoyed. There'll be a hot time in the old town tonight, I figured. But when she put on Maria Callas, the *Mad Scene* aria from *Il Pirata* and broke out the peach brandy, things started to go off on a strange tangent.

Cooking together and drinking together is what we always did. It was very comfortable. We both loved to cook and we both liked to get sloshed. And of course Diamanta always had to be half in the bag before we got down to the lovey-dovey stuff. It took a lot of alcohol to melt that cold Spanish heart. But tonight was different. It was my coming-home party, and it was also Diamanta's birthday. And then there was the peach brandy.

We were standing in the kitchen. Diamanta handed me a water glass. It was half full.

"Salud!"

"So we're drinking it straight?"

"Fuck no! I diluted it with vodka. Bottoms up!"

The kitchen was filled with delightful smells. A marinated leg of lamb was roasting in the oven. The gravy was bubbling on the stove.

"The lamb's ready to come out. Will you do the honors?"

I took the fragrant, sizzling leg of lamb out of the oven and put it on a platter. We carried the rest of the dishes to the dining room table: mashed potatoes, gravy, guacamole, petite peas, hot rolls and creamed onions.

The dogs were pacing like famished hyenas, and every time Callas hit a high note one of them would give out with an eerie moan.

The phone rang.

"Don't answer it. It's probably my mother."

More peach brandy. Diamanta was in a playful mood. She snatched up a can of Coolwhip and sprayed it in my face.

"You little stinker!"

I chased Diamanta around the dining room table and pelted her with handfuls of petite peas. The dogs followed, nipping at our heels. Diamanta scooped up a big gob of mashed potatoes, pushed it in my face and burst into peals of hysterical laughter. I caught her and dumped hot lamb gravy on top of her head. We were both giddy, crazed, silly-drunk.

Just then the doorbell jangled. It was the guy from the bakery with the cheesecake. He sure got an eyeful.

"We're looped, aren't we? Sozzled! Stinko!"

"Drunker than seven hundred dollars!"

Diamanta picked up the cheesecake.

"I always wanted to do this. The pies, you know? The old time movies?"

I puckered up my eyes. "You're gonna throw it in my face?"

"No, you do it to me!" She handed me the cheesecake. I smacked her in the face with it. I had to laugh. She looked exactly like a baby panda.

"Happy birthday!"

"Oh, my God, I forgot the carrots!"

"The carrots?"

"Rosemary carrots. You can't have leg of lamb without rosemary carrots."

Diamanta put me to work paring the carrots. She stood there watching me with a sly smirk on her face. She was crocked to the gills.

"That's making me horny as hell."

"What is?"

"That carrot. The way you're stroking it. It looks like it's growing."

She hopped up on the table, threw open her fur coat and spread her legs. "Oh, God, shove it up me!"

I quickly dropped my pants.

"No, the *carrot!* Fuck me with your carrot!"

I dipped the tip of my carrot in mint jelly and gingerly spread the little lips with my thumb and forefinger.

"Oh, my God…"

"How does it feel?"

"Cold. It feels cold. And bony, sort of."

"Bony? What do you mean, bony?"

"I don't know. Bony. Just bony. It feels like…like a skeleton's pecker."

Callas was going off like gangbusters. Her towering voice filled the room. "*Oh, s'io potessi dissipar le nubi!*" The dogs were chewing at my ankles.

"Now put some of that guacamole on my tits. Oh, yeah, like that. *Yeah, baby!* Spread it around. Oh, God, that feels so good. Oh, baby…"

Enough of this foolishness. I climbed up on the table and draped Diamanta's legs over my shoulders. But my foot got stuck in the gravy boat and then the table collapsed and we hit the deck. The leg of lamb went skidding across the floor with the snarling dogs in hot pursuit. Diamanta was convulsed with laughter. She had petite peas in her hair and her Russian sable fur coat was matted with creamed onions and mashed potatoes. I could hear the dogs crunching up the lamb bones…

Then there was the thing with the mocking bird. Mocking birds are extraordinary vocalists, and they're very territorial. One of these little songsters had staked out the Castle as his stomping ground, and he graced us every night with a performance that was at first enchanting and then excruciating.

Perched on top of a light pole next to the house, this guy perfectly imitated every oriole, robin, thrush and chickadee within a hundred miles, an amazing routine that took better than twenty minutes to complete. Then he'd start over, take it from the top, always with unflagging enthusiasm. He was tireless, a demon for work. He sang all night long. And it wasn't just the warbling of popular songbirds that comprised his routine. He'd do a telephone ringing, so real you'd reach for the phone, and a woodpecker's staccato tapping, and a whining dog that sounded exactly like Diamanta's wolfhound, Saluki.

Diamanta, always a light sleeper, was beside herself.

"I can't take much more of this," she complained one morning after a sleepless night. She had black circles around her eyes. "You've got to do something."

I tried pitching rocks at the bird. He'd fly off, but he always came back. I tried to imagine how he must have felt, this virtuoso performer. He was probably muttering to himself, "What a crock of shit. You go out there and give it everything you've got and they fucking throw rocks at you!"

It got worse and worse. He added a coyote howl to his routine, and that woke the dogs up and set them off barking their lungs out.

Diamanta was frantic. "He's gotta go," she told me. "Jerzy, I mean it. He's gotta go. I can't take it anymore."

The writing was on the wall. I was elected, of course. I wasn't happy about it. We borrowed a bolt action .22 with a telescopic sight from a neighbor—a "varmint" rifle he called it. There was no way out for me now.

It was a Tuesday night and the dogs were pacing frantically as if they knew something was up. While Diamanta pretended to do the dishes, I sat at the kitchen table loading the clip with the hollow point bullets the neighbor had given me. Less collateral damage, he'd said, with the hollow points. Jesus Christ, what a world!

Diamanta poured the Smirnoff's. "Please don't hate me," she murmured.

A full moon was shining bright as day as I stepped out the kitchen door into the back yard. I could tell by the way the gun felt in my hands that I wasn't going to miss.

"It's business," I told myself. It didn't help.

Now I had that little shit in the crosshairs. "Motherfucker," I whispered, "you brought this on yourself." That didn't help either.

I started to squeeze the trigger and suddenly he flew off. This actually happened. He bolted, in a flurry of feathers. And he didn't come back, as before. Not the next night or the next or the next. I know this sounds incredible, but It's true, every word. And what a break for me! I've done enough rotten things in my life without adding the cold-blooded murder of a songbird to my rap sheet.

A week later I met my trainer, Charlie Neighbors, in the Montebello OC drivers' lounge. We went out to our tractor and checked the in-cab satellite. They'd given us long miles—Barstow to Baton Rouge, with a stopover at the Schneider OC in West Memphis. First we had to pull an empty trailer up to the Fontana drop lot, pick up thirty-seven thousand pounds of coat hangers—a light load—and then we'd head up to Barstow and get on I-40 going east.

Charlie Neighbors was an excellent driver and a very

decent guy. After our first day on the road he declared that he was perfectly comfortable snoozing in the sleeper while I steered and geared. We did the Baton Rouge turnaround and stopped again at the West Memphis OC on the backside, then we dropped a trailer at Fontana and picked one up for Portland, and then we ran up to Seattle. Next it was back down to Portland, and over to Laramie, Fort Collins and Denver, and then we got a load out of Denver for Santa Monica, which took us right back into Montebello.

Charlie showed me my evaluation sheet. My grades were excellent. I'd been over several of the major passes without any problem—Donner, Shasta, Ashland, Tehachapi, and the Grapevine, of course, several times. We shook hands in the drivers' lounge. I now had a one-week interval on salary before my review and final road test. But before I left Montebello I got a call from Diamanta asking me to vacate for a few days because "her Mom" was flying in from Barcelona and would be staying at the Castle. She was in a dither and couldn't hustle me out fast enough. And I wasn't to call, either, until she announced that the coast was clear.

So I went to the Motel 6 in Carlsbad near the flower fields. Just for laughs the next day I took a drive by the Castle in Bonsall and there was a red Porsche with Mexican plates parked in the driveway behind the Snow Queen's car. The message was clear. The Alpha Male had arrived and I had been banished from the Ice Palace along with Gary and Daryl. When the lion returns to the kill, the jackals and hyenas scatter.

For SPQ the company put me up at the Ramada Inn in Montebello. SPQ consisted of five days of classroom review and testing on stuff like pre-trip inspection, four-point check, bump and run, power downshift, and so on, and then a final road test.

I passed everything, but not swimmingly. I was nervous when it came to the road test. Who wouldn't be with a guy with a clipboard lurking in the jump seat? I had to get into a strange tractor, different transmission, different engine, different tach speeds. I missed several gears and dragged my tandem duals over a curb. But I passed, and my training days were over. I was ready to move on to C-Team, running forty-eight states and Canada.

Not everyone passed, and those who failed the final road test were "sentenced" to an additional week of running Los Angeles with a trainer and hauling railroad containers.

My roommate at the Ramada Inn was Long To, a naturalized citizen from Vietnam. His village had been napalmed by U.S. forces during the war. Long To took a lot of ragging from the guys. They reversed his name and called him "Too Long."

"Hey, I know why you never have any girlfriends, Bro. *Too Long!* Too Long! Why, hell, you'd half kill the poor girl!"

This Too Long business was to them the absolute epitome of knee-slapping humor and a never-ending source of hilarity. It was repeated a dozen times a day. Long took it perfectly in stride, always cheerful and serene, a real bodhisattva. And so I was delighted when Long asked me if I wanted to be his partner for C-Team.

On our last day, there was a graduation ceremony and pizza and we all got Schneider National hats. Long and I met our STL (Schneider Team Leader), Grady Davis, a former Marine captain. Due to an acute shortage of tractors, Grady informed us, we would now have to wait for three weeks or a month for a power unit. We'd go home on salary and wait to be called. Then we'd either fly or drive a rental car to Harrisburg or to West Memphis to pick up our tractor. I shook hands with Long and we exchanged phone numbers.

No sooner did I get back to the Castle than Diamanta informed me that I'd be house-sitting and taking care of the wolfhounds while she flew to El Paso to be with her

Mom who was coming in once again from Barcelona. There was also a mysterious FedEx package which would be arriving from either Cartagena or Iquitos. I wasn't to open the package, she cautioned, but I had to watch closely for it. The package never arrived.

Just before I left for C-team I took Diamanta to the champagne brunch at the nearby upscale Pala Mesa Resort, where, romantic idiot that I was, I asked her to marry me. I thought the champagne and canapés might melt the ice around her cold Spanish heart, but she said her life was far too complicated to even consider marriage. She did promise, however, to ride with me after C team when I started running solo, and this now became my dream, my *raison d'etre*, the vision of the two of us tooling cross country in a condo conventional with an eight-foot ceiling, double bunk, refrigerator-freezer, built-in microwave, shower, pull-out work table and Dolby stereo system.

Back at the Montebello OC, I met Long To in the drivers' lounge. Grady Davis, our STL, put us in a rental car and sent us to West Memphis to pick up our power unit. It was a battered and dented '91 International Navistar cabover with eight hundred thousand miles on it. The sleeper was a hole in the wall, but it had cruise control and jake brakes, and it had deer whistles mounted below the west coast mirrors, and best of all, it was ours.

Before we left out we took a taxi downtown and we walked Beale Street, birthplace of the blues—seamy, touristy, historic—past BB King's Blues Club and other dives. I dipped my fingers in the Mississippi River and we hit for Jenks, Oklahoma, outside of Tulsa, and then we pulled twenty-five thousand pounds of toilet paper to Fontana.

It's a funny thing… All along I-40, through Arizona and California, you see signs like "Next Exit, Historic Route #66!" You get over to Barstow, and here's where the 1-40 ends. It splits up into the 215 and the I-15. Without any fanfare or ceremony or anything. Not even so much as adios, I-40, or thank you, I-40, or good-bye, I-40. Two thousand five hundred and forty-seven miles, Wilmington to Barstow, and they don't say shit. Instead, they're talking all crazy about the Mother Road, about the glory days of Route #66, about a road that's been officially closed since 1977. But I suppose it's like painters and writers. You have to be dead for a hundred years or so before they'll make a fuss over you.

We had a holiday layover and spent Thanksgiving Day at the Comfort Inn in Shelby, Montana. We ate Thanksgiving dinner at the Town Pump Truck Stop, just $6.00 all-you-can-eat for truck drivers.

I called and left Diamanta a Happy Thanksgiving message, and I also sent her a Comfort Inn postcard from Shelby. In the morning we picked up a load of Canadian peat moss bound for a mushroom farm in Salem, Oregon. Then it was Missoula, Spokane, Seattle, Tacoma, Portland and Salem for Long and myself, and then over to Reno.

I called my message number, but there was nothing from Diamanta. I knew by now that I was spinning my wheels with the Snow Queen. How could a poor truck driver possibly compete with a dentist who drives a Porsche and probably deals cocaine? Diamanta was playing with my affections. How long could I go on denying it? I was just there to blow up her tires while she waited for Bruno to return or while the two of them waited for that shoebox from Peru. Still, I couldn't let go.

At Wells, Nevada, on the 93, we heard the girls on the CB advertising the La Hacienda Sugar Shack brothel: "Free conversation, no obligation."

We passed the place at the 15-93 turnoff, all lit up like a Christmas tree. I wanted to go inside and take a peek at the Loreleis, but Long was too shy. "I am still married man, Mister Jer-cee."

On Rogers Pass in Idaho we had to stop for an elk herd crossing the road in the snow near the Salmon River. We got down to Fontana, and from Fontana we went right back to Jenks and then headed back to the Shaky, this time on the I-44 turnpike—a toll road, but we made great time—right down to I-40 and west we go.

From Montebello we went up to Barstow and over to Baton Rouge with a stopover at the West Memphis OC on the backside. We hit a terrific electrical storm in Memphis as we left out at night, rain in Arkansas and Oklahoma, and stars over Winslow as we switched drivers at a rest area at 2:00 a.m., huge brilliant stars, so much closer than in California, and the highway was littered with road-killed coyotes as we crossed the Painted Desert at dawn.

The Qualcomm Star-Serv in-cab computer system was a pain in the ass. Hundreds of abbreviations for macros, almost a separate esoteric language you had to learn. DWNTN for downtown, DPHK for drop and hook, OOR for out of route, the letter "Y" for why, and so on. We wasted half our time trying to decipher the messages and often we ended up having to call in to our STL to find out what the hell they were talking about. Why not just take a few minutes and spell everything out in the first place?

Our STL, Grady Davis, the ex-Marine captain, was a halfway decent guy—for an officer. At Schneider, all of the STLs were former military officers. They were used to moving men around on a chessboard, and that's exactly what they did.

Let's say you get a load out of LA for Baton Rouge. Pretty good, right? You go up to Barstow and you get on the 1-40 and away you go, Barstow to Memphis and down to Baton Rouge. Once you get on the Interstate all you have to think about is scales, truck stops and rest stops. It's tenth gear all the way.

Then you get over to Little Rock and your computer goes *beep* and you pull off at a rest area and take a look. It's a drop message. "Drop your trailer at the West Memphis OC and pick up trailer #612876. Proceed to the Schneider OC at Milton, Ontario."

Milton, Ontario. That's Ontario, Canada. You don't have your winter clothes, and you've already called your friends in New Orleans. You're just a number. They move you around on the chessboard like a dog soldier. You don't count.

Long To was without question the nicest guy I ever met. It's close quarters in a cabover, and fights between team drivers are legendary in the trucking business. I can honestly tell you that in the six months we spent together on the road Long never spoke one cross word to me, nor was there ever any word of complaint. He was patient and considerate and didn't gossip about the other drivers or badmouth the instructors. Long was separated from his wife and child, and his mother in Vietnam was slowly dying of cancer. All this must have been very painful for him, but he didn't bring his pain to the job.

Our schedule: five and five. You drive five hours, then you go in the sleeper for five hours. That's it. The rig keeps moving. A stop in a brake inspection area or a rest area to relieve oneself—fifteen minutes at the most. There are the fuel stops, of course, and we eat and take a shower

We'd walk out of a truck stop after breakfast and Long would climb up into the driver's seat. Before driving his shift he'd place his baby daughter's photo on the dash. I'd go into the sleeper. Soon it would be my turn. Even though I was asleep, I was aware of every modulation in the sound of the engine. I knew what gear he was in at every moment. I'd hear him downshifting as he went up a grade. If he slowed for a rest area, I'd have my shoes on before he parked.

One morning I awoke with a start. Long was freewheeling in ninth, endlessly it seemed, and the engine brakes weren't engaged. A long grade, I figured; maybe he was asleep at the wheel. I sat up, pulled the curtains aside and peered out. We were on Cajon Pass, going down into Victorville, and Long was wide awake, perfectly in charge.

Our meal tickets, left over from ADT and SPQ, were

good at all Schneider OC's. My favorite OC was West Memphis, where they served wonderful greasy southern food like grits and bacon and cornbread, collard greens, fried okra, hush puppies and fried chicken.

The yard at West Memphis, unlike the cramped quarters at Montebello, had plenty of room for truck parking. You got your key for your shower and while you were waiting you went though the line for your chow. The bathrooms were excellent, with lots of space, needle-spray showers, and wall heaters.

When you finished your shower you dropped your towel in the towel deposit and trundled out into the yard to where your rig was parked. You dove into the sleeper and conked out, certain in your mind that the morning would bring scrambled eggs with bacon and grits and sausage gravy.

What I liked best at West Memphis when I was falling asleep or just waking up was the symphony of industrial sounds that was somehow soothing and reassuring, the truck engines turning over, a generator chugging somewhere, the clatter of a freight going by, and the solemn, rhythmic clanking of a distant pile driver, like a beating heart. You were part of a living cosmos, a cosmos of work, and there was an order to it, and a purpose.

Long and I ran together for another month, then when Long flew to Vietnam for his mother's funeral, I began running solo, first out of Montebello and then out of the Fontana drop lot.

Alone on the road I looked forward to a decent meal and a good sleep. By a decent meal I mean that you finally get to a truck stop where you choke down the meatloaf and the mashed potatoes and the gravy, or the double cheeseburger and fries, or the trucker-sized breakfast with the twelve eggs, the forty-leven pancakes and the oceans of coffee.

The rest stops at night were a beacon of lights, a perfect place to jungle up. I'd pull into a spot between two eighteen-wheelers, nod at the other drivers, sometimes do a little palaver with them. Parked between Covenant and England, or between Swift and JB Hunt, I felt perfectly safe.

When morning came I'd hear them taching up on all sides. They were getting ready to pull out. I'd pile out of my cab, thinking about coffee. The neighboring drivers would be out there, swaggering around their rigs, spanking their tires, doing a pre-trip inspection. I'd go back and piss on my duals. I couldn't think of doing a pre-trip until I'd had breakfast, or at least coffee.

After breakfast I'd get out on the Interstate, and this was a breeze. I'd be pulling long miles, hauling for the other coast, an interval that afforded complete freedom, at least for the mind. Just keep the pedal to the metal and downshift once in a while for a grade.

When I pulled the Grapevine I always felt good. I was nearly home, for one thing. In the lanes beside me, as I chugged along at five miles an hour, were the other drivers, Werner, Old Dominion, Mayflower, or independents from all over the place. We were all going so slow that you could have a conversation out the window. It was chummy and also surreal.

At the top of Grapevine Hill, a brake inspection area and a truck stop. And a waitress named Betsy. For thousands of miles I'd look forward to seeing Betsy, the Waitress at the Top of Grapevine Hill. I didn't have any designs on her. It wasn't like that. She must have talked to a million truckers a day.

"I see from your shirt that you're a Schneider driver. Okay, sweetie, I'll be back with your guacamole."

I loved to watch Betsy balancing an armload of steaming plates, stoically enduring the wisecracks and deftly eluding the grubby hands of ass-pinching truck stop Romeos. Doing her job, smiling at everyone, flipping a little sassy backchat at the cook, keeping track of her customers. "Curly fries or the regular?"

"If you was to step in a pile of dog shit, what'd be the first thing you'd do—clean the shit off your shoes or go after the dog?" This was the question put to me by Attorney Benny "Hog" Wilde, at Trevor Llewellyn's annual Birthday Clambake in Fayetteville, New York.

It was early July and I had forty thousand pounds of Huggies in the trailer destined for Sears in Schenectady. As I was clearing Buffalo I got a message on the in-cab satellite from Grady Davis in Montebello, reminding me that Sears wouldn't be taking the delivery because of Independence Day, and I would have to lay over. Grady didn't have to twist my arm.

When I got over to Seneca Falls I pulled into the Nice-N-Easy Truck Stop off I-90 and called my ex-brother-in-law, Trevor Llewellyn. It turned out that I was just in time. Just in time, that is, for the Birthday Clambake.

Peaceful little Fayetteville! Where I got married for the first at the DeWitt Community Church. There was plenty of room to park my rig in front of the Big House on tree-lined Lilac Road. Trevor met me at the front door. It had been two years or more, but Trevor—sleek, salon-tanned and suave as ever—hadn't changed a bit. He was overjoyed to see me.

As we stood in the doorway embracing and talking I smelled the remembered musty dank-wood smell of the huge old place combined with the everlasting stink of Josh Llewellyn's cigars.

But now there was a new smell: *cat piss*. After his parents' passing, Trevor explained, he'd moved into the Big House, bringing with him his Rotweiller, Dumbo, and thirty-seven cats.

"Come on, JM," Trevor said, taking my battered canvas gym bag. We stepped into the hallway and headed up the stairs, "I'll show you to your room."

The first thing I did was hit the shower. I'd been on the road for twenty-eight days: Phoenix, Denver, Salt Lake,

Oakland, Tacoma, Seattle, and back south over Mount Shasta, Mount Ashland and the Grapevine, then the OC at Montebello again, and right out to Denver, Chicago, the Big Apple and Buffalo— nine thousand miles all told.

I stepped out of the shower and was going to return to my room, but Trevor's ogre of a Rotweiller was stationed outside the bathroom and growled savagely every time I tried to open the door. I banged on the floor and Trevor came up and locked the brute in one of the spare bedrooms.

"Sorry, JM," Trevor said, handing me a gin and tonic. "It takes Dumbo a while to get used to people. It's a pity you can't stay with us longer."

I got dressed and went down to the kitchen. Trevor freshened up my drink, then we went to the sunroom so I could meet "the children." Marie Llewellyn, Lance's mother, had been a landscape painter of some repute. The sunroom was her studio. In the old days it smelled of oil paint and turpentine, and it was the one room in the Big House where I felt at home.

Now the sunroom was full of cats. Trevor cautiously opened the sliding glass door and we quickly stepped inside, gliding the door shut behind us. The cats thronged around us, meowing and rubbing against our legs. The stink made my eyes water. There were litter boxes everywhere, and cats were perched on the furniture, gazing at us with grave expressions and round staring eyes. A line from *Isaiah* was going through my head. *And their houses shall be full of doleful creatures…*

A big gray brute leaped up on a divan and began to retch. He upchucked on a red satin pillow and Trevor grabbed a towel.

"Oh, Puffy! Poor baby! That's Puff Daddy. He's got an upset stomach. It's been going on for weeks. The vet says he may have gingivitis."

We went out and strolled around the grounds. It was a tremendous relief to fill my lungs with fresh air. We visited the gardener's cottage, the tool shed where the Gravely was kept, then the pool and the bathhouse. On the wall in the bathhouse was a photo of Josh "Lucky" Llewellyn driving the Gravely, clamping his cigar, flashing that golden Attorney Lucky Llewellyn Grin.

"Thanks for all your postcards, by the way, JM. Boy, you sure get around! Come on, let's go around front and see if anybody's here yet. How's your drink?"

The clams and the kegs arrived along with the catering crew from Hinnerwattle's Grove. A black Lincoln pulled onto the front lawn and two men in plaid Bermudas and black silk knee socks got out.

"Come on over here, JM. I want you to meet a couple of Dad's law partners. JM—Jerzy Mulvaney—this is Attorney Dan Danheisser."

A small oily man with sharp features grabbed my hand: "Attorney Dan Danheisser—Shallowsteps, Shumpert, Snick, Gallup, Gortner and Gumbel." Then Trevor introduced me to the other guy: "Benny, this is my ex-brother-in-law and dearest friend, Jerzy Mulvaney. JM, Dad's law partner, Attorney Benny Wilde."

"Call me Hog. Hog Wilde. That's what they call me. Hog Wilde. So you're Jerzy Mulvaney, eh? From California, I understand."

A couple of odd ducks, these two. Men of the world, certainly, yet curiously ingenuous, like underdone croissants that had come out of the oven too soon.

"Do you know Stephen King personally?"

"Well, no…I haven't…met him."

"How about Stephen Spielburg? You *do* live in Hollywood."

"More like Los Angeles, actually."

"LA, Hollywood, same thing. Do you know Martin Scorcese? How about John Malkovich?"

"Jesus, Hog! Give the man a chance to answer the question, will you? You're not cross-examining a witness, you know!"

"Okay, Danny Boy—you go ahead and ask a question. Your witness,

Counselor!"

"Okay, JM, tell me this—is Charlie Sheen really as *wild* as they say?"

The catering people had fired up the grill. You could smell sausages sizzling. Attorney Hog Wilde raised his foaming plastic beer cup.

"Look at us, will ya! Sir Trevor, Danny Boy, JM and yours truly, Hog Wilde! The Four Musketeers! Let's tap that keg. What do you say? Drinks all around for the Four Musketeers! Happy Birthday, Sir Trevor! Jeez, what a day! I just wish your dad and Ziggy Shallowsteps were here to see this. But, say, JM, let's talk about literature. Tell me, what do you think of *The Sun Also Rises?*"

"I haven't read it."

"Fascinating! Say, we'll have to talk about this again some time. Can you shuck clams, JM?"

"That I can do, Benny."

"Hog! Call me Hog…"

In the morning I took my coffee out to a bench next to the gardener's cottage and caught up on my trucker's log. Trevor joined me with his coffee and Kahlua.

"Right there in that cottage is where I lost my cherry. Cindy Lo Bianco, the gardener's daughter. She's got six kids now. Married some Mafia putz."

After my delivery at Sears in Schenectady, I sent a request for TAH (Time At Home) to Grady Davis in Montebello. *Get me back to the Shaky!* I went up to Montreal, then down to Detroit, over to KC, then Jenks, Wichita Falls, Houston and Las Cruces.

I called my message number again and again. There was nothing from Diamanta. Consumed with jealous fantasies, I left several impatient messages on her machine, and then, at Deming, I left an angry message demanding that she at least grant me the courtesy of a response.

As I was coming off the Chiriaco Summit on 1-10 east

of Coachella and Indio, I finally got a message from Diamanta: "I don't remember making you any promises. Did you really think I was in love with you? We were friends, nothing more. Goodbye, Jerzy!"

I continued on to Colton, and then, instead of going to Montebello, I took the 215 down to Temecula. I knew it was stupid, but I had to see for myself, so I dropped down to the 78 and headed for Bonsall. I played Diamanta's message again: "We were friends, nothing more." The emphasis was on the word "were", it seemed to me. When I got to Bonsall, sure enough, Bruno's red Porsche was squatting in the driveway.

Goodbye, Jerzy!

I parked my rig a block away from the Castle and got down from the cab. Should I go up and ring the doorbell? Should I confront her? Suddenly, Attorney Benny Wilde's words of wisdom came back to me: "If you was to step in a pile of dog shit, what'd be the first thing you'd do—clean the shit off your shoes or go after the dog?" Well, I'd stepped in the shit, all right. No doubt about that. And there didn't seem to be much sense in going after the dog, so I climbed back into my battered Navistar cabover, found second gear, and headed due west to dear old Motel 6.

7

I went into something of a slump after that, I admit it. I took a leave of absence from Schneider and didn't do much of anything except moon around like an idiot. And extend my leave of absence and extend it again. It was good to be back in LA, but I was plenty nervous at first about the way I'd skipped out on M'Butu from Mogadishu that time in Miami. Then, a week later, I heard through the grapevine that the ogre had been deported, and that put my fears to rest. I moved into a vintage 1920's house on Sonrisa Street with two Tongans in a sweetly decaying neighborhood of narrow cracked sidewalks, slanting porches, battered old cars, and everywhere the smell of onions frying. A white fence that was missing several pickets surrounded my house, and a creaking weathervane perched on the roof would spin crazily when a breeze rattled the dry brown beards of the palms. The Tongans spoke (or pretended to speak) no English, but they were amiable enough, and I loved my white picket fence with its gap-toothed smile and the beautiful green lawn grass that grew knee high and sprouted lovely little yellow bells. I didn't think about Diamanta. I didn't think about anything. I'd sit on my front porch with a 40-ounce King Cobra and watch the hopeful ice cream man pushing his rickety jingle cart, and two tawny next-door cats that rolled and slept in the fleecy green grass like a pair of leopards lounging in the heart of an emerald forest.

I have to say that Schneider was more than patient with me, more than fair. But then it was in their interest to be fair, to keep me on at any cost. There's a ninety-nine percent turnover in the trucking industry. It's no picnic out there. It's a hard life.

It wasn't true, what I said about Diamanta, that I didn't think about her. I did think about her, of course, not in any sense of trying to figure out what exactly had brought about my descent from significant other to insignificant other, but just remembering the good times, like the day we first met, at the champagne brunch at the Downtown Sheraton in LA. There's nothing like that first glass of ice-cold champagne—clean, crisp, bubbly—to take your breath away. In an instant you're giddy drunk and it seems that anything is possible and life really is a midsummer night's dream. The second glass brings you down and you spend the rest of the morning chasing that airy-fairy feeling. But I guess Puck, or Robin Goodfellow, or whatever you want to call him really did put the magic juice on my eyelids, because I went gaga over Diamanta right then and there. Later on, of course, the little stinker got around to his real work, which was transforming me into a donkey.

Finally, at Sonrisa Street, I started working on a screenplay based on the characters that hung out at the Angel's Camp Tavern back in New York—Hal Feldman, of course, Tequila Lil, Parcifal the Poet, flower lady Raggedy Ann with her bunch of wilted carnations and her Long Island Ice Tea, and halfway pretty Brenda Boudreau, vodka martini, three olives.

Then one day out of the blue the sculptor Bronco Childress called me from Paris asking if I'd like to spend a month or two at his newly formed artist colony at Belle Isle, the Louisiana plantation where Lady Mariska and I had stopped over after fleeing from Big Bill Sturdyvant's Pinacolada Bar in Miami. I said yes, I'd be delighted, and the next day I boarded a Greyhound bus bound for New Iberia. I brought along my screenplay, "Angels Camp."

At Belle Isle I checked in with Tootsie Feinschriber, the new owner, a hugely successful author of romance novels and a dedicated patron of the arts. Bronco, I learned, would be arriving any day now. It had been pretty grubby on the bus, but I was feeling optimistic because I knew it would be first cabin from here on out. Writer in residence! I was excited. Getting dumped by Diamanta had pretty much taken the wind out of my sails, and this Belle Isle deal, I figured, was exactly the boost I needed to get me back up and running.

There had been some changes since my first visit to Belle Isle, I discovered. The slave dwellings had been completely refurbished on the inside, each with a bathroom, kitchenette and air conditioning, to house artist colony residents and also the tourists who would be flocking to Belle Isle to watch Bronco work on his colossal, welded steel and cast bronze *Gigantopithecus*.

Right after I moved into Belle Isle I made extensive repairs to the replica Manneken Pis fountain, the Pissing Boy. The repairs, which involved digging out and replacing a leaking section of PVC, made me feel useful and also endeared me to Tootsie Feinschriber, our in-house literary diva. I did some grunt work in the Peach Orchard, pruning and watering, and eventually I was tasked with the editing of the Grand Dame's manuscripts. I'd sit reverently at Tootsie Feinschriber's feet while Tootsie—propped up with pillows, wrapped in her shawl, surrounded by her many and much-corrected manuscripts—reclined on the four-poster antebellum bed in the "Mathilda Bedroom," the room in which Mariska and I had slept on my first visit to Belle Isle. Balancing her teacup, peering over her bifocals, tapping a manuscript page, she'd fix me with a bright, birdlike eye: "Soo…Dollink, how do you like my latest...*extravaganza?*"

On the day I arrived Tootsie Feinschriber held a little soiree on the verandah so I could meet the other inmates. We were two writers, a painter named Kristof, a surly Polish sculptor, Stasic or Stasig, no English, and an interpretive dancer, Alessandra, a big leggy girl with brown bangs and big square teeth, a real centauress. My slave cabin was next door to hers.

My new home was very comfortable, I'll say that. But sometimes at night when I was asleep I had the eerie feeling that my shack was meandering around the property—particularly in Alessandra's direction—like Baba Yaga's magical hut mounted on chicken legs. And there were ghosts... The ghost of Jean Lafitte, for example, and the ghost of Mathilda, the Creole slave girl whose portrait hung on the wall of Tootsie Feinschriber's bedroom.

Valentin, the other writer, was a Yale graduate and a certified black belt schizophrenic. He was on the dole. You have to be bright to be crazy, and Valentin was both. Trading on his charm and erudition, he'd attached himself to Tootsie Feinschriber eons ago. This I learned from Alessandra. We'd have our little confabs near Bronco's half finished concrete boat in the Peach Orchard. Valentin had subsisted for decades in a parasitic manner, Alessandra informed me, a tumor clinging to the wall of Tootsie Feinschriber's uterus. He was a cockroach, Valentin, a literate insect. Where Tootsie was all sparkle, charisma and pizzazz, Valentin was passive, analytical, phlegmatic. As far as anyone knew, the man had never held a job. Alessandra did say that he'd once published a philosophical treatise on the importance of being indigent.

There was something almost reptilian about Valentin. He dressed like a European hoodlum. Nearly every day you'd see him reclining on a meditation bench in the sun near the Manneken Pis fountain, his eyes covered by black plastic eyecups. His boyish white body glistened with baby oil, and his maroon Speedo trunks left little to the imagination. From time to time he'd nervously run a hand through his flowing mane of silvery gray hair. Always at his side was a dog-eared copy of *Being and Nothingness*.

The artist today, Valentin was fond of asserting, has completely outlived his usefulness. The world, he insisted, no longer needs artists, poets, seers. The world needs people who are not afraid to spill blood. He was dead right, of course, but what you have to understand is that Valentin was forever talking about the plight of the artist. Valentin thought he was an artist, but he wasn't. He was an intellectual. What Valentin needed in order to transform him into an artist was fifteen or sixteen years in a steel mill.

The day after I finished the repairs on the Manneken Pis fountain, the painter, Kristof—dapper in his bullfighter's beret, tweed sport jacket and smock—emerged, brush in hand, from his cabin on the other side of Alessandra's hut. He stood on his doorstep, gazing meditatively at the gurgling fountain.

"Ah, the cherub is pissing in the pool once again," he murmured. "It's a good omen."

I discovered a beautiful word one day as I was poking around in Tootsie Feinshriber's huge library. *Sprezzatura*, a word pertaining to art and life in the Italian High Renaissance. Aristocrats wanted to possess *sprezzatura*, and artists strove to depict it. As discussed in Baldassare Castiglione's *Book of the Courtier*, *sprezzatura* was a reflection of the Renaissance man as both a graceful performer and a superficial manipulator. According to Count Ludovico, a character in the book: "*Sprezzatura* is an art which does not seem to be an art. One must avoid affectation and practice in all things a certain *sprezzatura*, disdain or carelessness, so as to conceal art, and make whatever is done or said appear to be without effort and almost without any thought about it."

Kristof had *sprezzatura*, no question about it. And Tootsie Feinshriber, sure, she had it. And Bronco, of course, Bronco was absolutely loaded with it. Bronco was crawling with *sprezzatura*.

As if to prove the point, a day or so before Thanksgiving Bronco returned to Belle Isle, fresh from his triumphant one man show in Paris, and the place began to ring with the thunderous blows of Thor's hammer as the demigod slugged away at his colossal Gigantopithecus. Bronco was in a euphoric mood as always, but he was also up in arms about a *Rolling Stone Magazine* article in which some journalist had referred to him as an "*arriviste*."

"Bronco Childress is no *arriviste*," Tootsie told me one morning as I sat at her feet in the Mathilda Bedroom. "Bronco Childress is a colossus. He's a continent. It is we who are *arrivistes*. We are new arrivals on the shores of a continent called Bronco Childress. To say that Bronco has charisma is putting it mildly. Bronco has an additional something. He has…"

"*Sprezzatura?*"

"Precisely!" Tootsie said with a delighted chuckle. "You've been reading Castiglione, I see. Very good! In Bronco Childress we see the artist in full panoply. Gigantopithecus, the largest primate that ever lived, with its great mouth of grinding molars, is a manifestation of Bronco's formidable appetite for life, of his prodigious capacity to masticate and devour. His next sculpture, *Deinonychus the Raptor*, will express his swiftness, his savagery, his sagacity…"

I knew I should have been working on my screenplay, but instead an immense lethargy consumed me. It was, of course, a touch of post-traumatic stress syndrome in the wake of Diamanta's abrupt dismissal. She'd played Donkey Kong with my affections, no question about it. This intense torpor was a continuation and escalation of the ennui that had possessed me in the white picket fence world of Sonrisa Street, but now the friendly jingle of the ice cream vendor's hopeful pushcart had given way to a menacing chorus of fever cannons and Congo tom toms booming deep in the heart of darkness. There was no escaping it, this lethargy, no avoiding it. The muggy, mosquito-infested heat of Belle Isle was a presence that bludgeoned me with a padded hammer. Brownish rain drizzled down from a sluggish sky, warm as baby drool and fragrant with honeysuckle nectar, tucking me in, rocking me to sleep, filling my ears with a deadening lullaby. The birds grew silent, and as angry storm clouds hammered the overarching live oaks down into the prehistoric ooze of the swamp, I felt myself sinking with them into a black pool of weariness. I slept and slept, for hours, days, while fever images chased each other in my brain. I'd wake up only to answer the call of nature, after which I'd tramp out to the edge of the bayou where I'd sit on a rotting log and peer into a shadow-world where light and darkness flirted like fireflies and nothing was distinguishable, neither land nor water, everything intermingled, a pancake world of mosquitoes and catcalls and mirage.

Bronco was a prince, I have to say that. He took me to Clancy's in New Orleans for soft shelled crabs, and then to the French Quarter jazz clubs, and finally to the strip joints—Big Daddy's, Bourbon Street Burlesque and the Can Can Cabaret. It was intoxicating, sure, going to the places with a celebrity, with a guy who was Mr. *Sprezzatura* himself, but even the red carpet treatment, the sparkling meals and the naked pole-dancing girls couldn't rouse me from my torpor. All I could see when I closed my eyes was a black sun rising in a sea of blood. The world—a basketful of lecherous crabs—what did I want with it?

A few days later Bronco introduced me to film director Sergey Billetnikov, who optioned my screenplay for three hundred bucks after merely glancing at it. We had a little confab out in the Peach Orchard near Bronco's half finished concrete boat.

"I love your screenplay, I really do. But we need conflict. These two guys are brothers, right?"

"No, just friends," I managed.

"We'll make them brothers. They're both in love with the same woman, okay? Steinbeck, *East of Eden*. And one of them is a dwarf. Now where did that come from? You see? You see? David Mamet works this way, you know. He'll start with a scene, a few lines of dialog... I've got this image...this image of a dwarf riding a unicycle. With a parrot on his shoulder. It's a story of loss and redemption. Wait, I've got it. They're both dwarfs—or is it dwarves? Do you see where I'm going with this?"

"Yeah...sure...yeah." I was weary, bleary, only half there. Every word was an effort, but I knew I had to pretend an interest. After all, this was my big break.

"Supernatural thriller meets coming of age meets classic buddy film. And just a touch of noir," Sergey went on, flashing his dimples. "Think *Papillon* meets the *Wizard of Oz*. Gritty but light. Don't ask me how I do it. I'm going on pure instinct here. When you're hot, you're hot! Now, tell me you understand. Tell me straight up and down. Tell me you see where I'm going with this. Make me believe it. I'm saying to you, Jerzy, can you write it? And you're saying to me, Sergey, can a fat baby fart? Loss and redemption, my friend. Now give it to me with both barrels! Can you write it?"

I gathered all my strength. "Can I write it? Can I write it? Sergey, can a fat baby fart? Loss and redemption, brother. Gritty but light!"

"Yeah, yeah...gritty-light...and a little touch of noir."

"*Lawrence of Arabia* meets *Pretty in Pink*?"

"Bring it!"

I was curious about Mathilda, and so was Alessandra. We conjectured that Mathilda's mother or grandmother had been brought to Louisiana from Senegambia, the West African slave trading center, and that Mathilda, fathered by a French plantation owner, had been born into slavery and probably spoke a patois similar to the patois spoken by Baptiste, our present day chef at Belle Isle Plantation, when he talked with Andre the dishwasher and Philippe the prep cook. One day the two of us were rummaging around in the attic and Alessandra discovered an old trunk filled with receipts, recipes and lists, including a Belle Isle Plantation April 1848 Inventory, which appraised Mathilda—"Creole Negress, age 19"—at $1,200. Mathilda must have been highly regarded because elsewhere in the Inventory it showed that the Belle Isle Plantation owner had purchased several slaves from nearby Chandler Oaks Plantation, a mother, a father and two children—a whole family—for just a under a grand.

A few days later we found Mathilda's grave, out in the Peach Orchard near Bronco's concrete boat. We picked some roses from the garden and placed them by her headstone, and somehow that made me feel better. It was as if I were putting roses on Diamanta's grave. I was starting to come back to life.

I got a call from Aunt Mizpah informing me that my mother had recently been recuperating in the big house at 61 Park Street after having one of her spells and spending two weeks at the asylum in Binghamton, and also that I would soon be getting a check from the estate of my great aunt Frieda Von Stauffel, a woman of whose existence I was entirely unaware. Pennies from heaven! I sent my mother a get-well card and began making plans for a rosy future—Europe, maybe, or even the trip to South America with Doyle Junghammer.

Now that Bronco had returned to Belle Isle, busloads of tourists with designer jeans and expensive cameras began arriving daily and all the slave cabins were full. Kristof had a show coming up in the Big Easy, the Polish sculptor had been deported and Tootsie Feinschriber had flown to New York to shlep her latest blockbuster. My screenplay was in tatters, thanks to the mad Russian, Sergey Billetnikov. I wanted to put Mathilda in the screenplay but Billetnikov wouldn't hear of it.

I started hanging out with Baptiste, the cook. He was a regular guy. We understood each other. We were cut from the same cloth: dishwashers, taxi drivers, machine gunners, we're the guys who sweep the floors, flip the burgers and fight the wars on the ground. The truth is that I would have been more comfortable working in the kitchen at Belle Isle than playing at being a writer in residence.

Baptiste had a pirogue, and we'd tool around the bayous. It was peaceful out there and the sky's reflection etched on the limpid black water was so clear we seemed to be floating on top of the clouds. The bayou was teeming with wild creatures—alligators, snakes and birds. You rarely saw them but you knew that they were there, slithering, creeping, stalking. They were busy catching and devouring one another. A slaughterhouse, yes, but it was slaughter waged in the name of hunger rather than on behalf of politics and religion, and there was something honest and refreshing about that. And every so often, just to keep things interesting, the ghost of Jean Lafitte would send a phantom cannon ball scudding across our bow.

Then there was the matter of Alessandra, the interpretive dancer. Baptiste had a crush on Alessandra. But who didn't? Of course we never had a chance, not me, and certainly not Baptiste. I mean, he wasn't much to look at—a couple of missing teeth in front, a blue stubble beard, a raffish glint in his eye.

Baptiste was a bull that you hit between the eyes with a hammer. He was stunned, mesmerized, drunk with the terror and wonder of Alessandra. Some nights we'd sit on the verandah with beers and watch her dancing in the Peach Orchard, dancing on Mathilda's grave, dancing in the sky. She'd peek over the horizon and wink at us, her huge moon-face lighting up the world as she ascended to the heavens. Alessandra wasn't a woman; she was a constellation. And when dawn sent Venus and the Pleiades scampering for cover, we'd watch her vanish into the west, riding the ecliptic, moving with the fixed stars.

We went to see a hoodoo lady named Madame Yvonne who lived in a shanty that crouched warily behind long silver-gray beards of Spanish moss. Baptiste thought maybe she could help him. She was supposed to be an expert at casting love charms. We had to travel by pirogue. Her shack was deep, deep in the bayou. The two of them talked the Creole patois. I didn't know what they were saying, but Baptiste spelled it all out for me on the way back to Belle Isle.

For Baptiste, Madame Yvonne filled a hollowed out apple with honey and the name "Alessandra" scrawled on a slip of paper, then sealed the apple up in a tin can and burned a candle on top of it. She also gave Baptiste a mojo bag filled with herbs and alligator teeth. None of it worked.

On our next visit Madame Yvonne prescribed a graveyard-dirt love spell, so we brought her some dirt from Mathilda's grave, and also, at Madame Yvonne's request, some dirt from one of Alessandra's footprints. Madame Yvonne filled a clay pot with Alessandra's footprint dirt and buried a rose quartz crystal, then planted marigolds in the pot and she made Baptiste eat some of the marigold blossoms. She wanted Baptiste to bring her a single hair from Alessandra's *chatte*, too. Now how the hell was he supposed to get that, can you tell me?

Things happened quickly after that. Bronco finished his concrete boat and sailed for Belize, a cellist from Minneapolis took over my cabin, Alessandra moved in with Valentin and Sergey Billetnikov tore up my option.

On the day before Bronco sailed I dropped by his studio to say goodbye. Bronco was putting the finishing touches on his terrifying life-size steel Gigantopithecus. He remarked that I was looking better, and we chatted for a while, then he showed me how to use a rebar bender. There's something very real and truly honest about a rebar bender. A person can believe in a rebar bender.

8

"*The jungle is dark but full of diamonds, Willy,*" Doyle Junghammer proclaimed as we hoisted beers at the Angels Camp Tavern one night after our workout. "Remember? You remember what Ben said in *Death of a Salesman?* When I was seventeen I walked into the jungle, and when I was twenty-one I walked out. And by God I was rich!"

Before we left for South America Doyle gave me his estranged wife's address and phone number—just in case "something happened"—and I gave Doyle Aunt Mizpah's number in Brandon. We drove to Key West, sold Doyle's car, caught a Colombian freighter to Rio and a plane to our jumping-off point, Brasilia, a city of fizzing potassium street lights. Quickly, we found a cheap hotel and set about the task of buying the necessary gear, machetes, an ax, hammocks, mosquito netting, shovels, picks, a two-man sluice-box and other mining equipment. In less than a day we had everything we needed, according to Doyle's calculations, and at an excellent price. It had all gone swimmingly. Flushed with confidence, we decided to take a week to get our bearings, study the maps, and have a little fun.

There was another reason for our stopover in Brasilia which I won't dwell on but I mention it because it's significant in the light of what later developed. Doyle, since our two-week voyage on the Colombian freighter, had been having stomach problems, and he wanted to take time out to see a doctor, and also to "get adjusted to the climate and the food." All in all we were two weeks in the bars and brothels of Brasilia. I should have taken this stomach business of Doyle's as an early omen that our venture was shot in the ass but I was caught up in the excitement of it and also I was perhaps too young to believe in omens.

We made the next leg of our journey on a riverboat carrying a cargo of kapok, tapir skulls, black balls of smoked rubber and half-cured caiman skins. Loaded with Indians, smiling children, dogs, pigs, pink orchids and mountains of mangoes, papayas and green bananas, the craft looked like a floating fruit salad. For a hundred miles we sailed the Araguaia River, a tributary of the Amazon, hugging the edge of the Mato Grosso, while flying fish vaulted out of the swirling chocolate water and flopped on deck.

In Maraba we found a guide, Lucien, a personable young Indian with a *bataloa*, a thirty-foot boat, and we were off again without delay, navigating the Xingu, the Tapajos, the Madeira, the Purus, and then the great Amazon itself.

We reached another stopping point some three weeks later near the confluence of the Rio Branco, the Rio Diablo and the Rio Negro, about 150 miles west of Manaus. There was a clearing in the jungle and a *savoropanco*, a thatched hut built by Indians that served as a shelter for fishermen and travelers. The gold fields, Lucien informed us, were now only a few miles distant.

Since the savoropanco was unoccupied, we decided to take a few days to sort through our gear, make plans and swim in the clear, slow-moving water. We spread out our gear in the savoropanco and strung up our hammocks. Lucien caught some large crayfish; the tails, when broiled, were every bit as good as lobster. Some Indian girls drifted out of the forest. They were curious, but shy at first. They brought us fruit; we gave them some *rapadura* and *gaseosas*, soft drinks. Before long they were sharing our hammocks. Making love for them was apparently as casual and natural a matter as shaking hands. At night we set out trotlines. One morning Doyle discovered that something had straightened one of his hooks. A *paiche*, Lucien informed us, or a *pirarucu*. The latter, he said, could easily reach the size of the *bataloa*. Intrigued, Doyle and I beefed up our tackle—stronger lines, bigger hooks, and we baited with a whole catfish. We were determined to catch one of these monsters.

All told it was a delightful idyll at the savoropanco with the girls, the fresh-caught fish, and the lazy days spent swimming and dozing on the *praia*, the riverbank. I was happy and Doyle was ecstatic. "*The jungle is dark but full of diamonds, Willy*," he kept repeating triumphantly.

As I looked back over our adventure I realized that the clichés I'd heard all my life about South America had recently become real and palpable, the slumbering volcanoes, the peaks wrapped in mist, the quicksand, the vampire bats, the rotting rope bridges, the crocodiles, the shrunken heads, the soldier ants, the snakes that suck women's milk at night, the lost temples, the fabulous black orchids, the *bandeirantes*... Yet, somehow, none of this—the harshness of it, I mean, the danger—had touched us. Thus far we'd carried it all off with ridiculous ease. We had traversed the Mato Grosso, the White Man's Grave, without incident. And now the gold fields were within striking distance. Once again, as I had during our sojourn in Brasilia, I experienced a premature sense of accomplishment. I thought of the cruel Spaniards who came to these lands to find El Dorado and to carry off Atahualpa's Treasure. They died as they had lived, by the sword, the jungle swallowed them up, and the lost treasure cities remained unfound. Could it be then that Doyle and I would succeed where men such as Francisco Pizarro and

Hernando de Soto had failed?

One evening after a few tots of rum Doyle and I decided to spend the night on the bataloa, which Doyle had re-christened the "Queen Midas," leaving Lucien in the savoropanco to guard the equipment and supplies. Drunk as we were, Doyle and I dutifully set out our baited lines, as we'd done on previous nights, then we retired. From the deck as I closed my eyes I could see the flickering light of Lucien's fire up at the savoropanco. Several hours later I awoke, feeling the river rushing beneath me. Something had changed. In the jungle you hear tales of rivers that rise overnight. Could this have been the case? I blinked my eyes. The twinkling light of Lucien's fire was gone, as was the familiar silhouette of the savoropanco. In the brilliant moonlight I saw a much narrower river. And we were moving. I reached for the mooring rope and pulled it in, with a clump of *cana brava*— wrenched up by the roots—attached. I shook Doyle awake. Then I noticed that one of our trotlines was taut and stretched well out in front of the bataloa. I grabbed the line and pulled. It felt as if we were hooked into a submarine. Then, as Doyle reached my side, we both saw a gigantic silvery flash as a great fish rolled some 300 feet in front of us in the moonlight.

"*Pirarucu*," Doyle whispered hoarsely. "Christ, that thing must weigh 500 pounds."

I unsheathed my machete and cut the line. Our forward motion slowed, but not by much since we were headed downstream, drifting with a swift-moving current. I grabbed a pole and tried to steer us in to shore while Doyle attempted to start the engine. The river was becoming shallower by the minute. I was afraid we were going to hit a rock. Ahead was a waterfall. I heard the engine cough but it was too late. I yelled at Doyle to jump, then I went over the side. There was a tremendous crunching sound of shattering timbers as the Queen Midas ran aground. I swam for the praia. Looking back I saw the

Queen Midas balanced on top of a rushing waterfall less than thirty feet high, her propeller clean out of the water. Doyle, who had ridden out the crash, was unhurt. He waved at me from the cabin, killed the engine and gave me a sardonic smile: "Ain't this some shit?"

The Queen Midas was gutted. We salvaged what few items we could, then started out on foot, following the river upstream, the object being to get back to the savoropanco, where our cache of supplies was stored. Since the river was constantly branching off into new tributaries, we had no way of knowing if we were even on the right river.

As night began to fall at the end of our third day's march we spotted a blue light up ahead in a little clearing. Thinking we'd run upon an Indian campsite, we cautiously approached, Doyle with his gun drawn. But there was no one. The strange blue light, which illuminated the whole grotto, emanated from a fungus that grew at the base of an enormous dead tree. Exhausted, we flung ourselves down in this eerie yet somehow friendly spot and fell dead asleep.

Hours later I was jolted awake by some instinct. An Indian was standing a few feet away from us, the blue light of the grotto glinting on his crossed cartridge belts.

"*Acu!*" I began (the standard jungle greeting and the only Indian word I knew).

"What does he want?" Doyle had awakened and had his gun out. The Indian, I noticed, had not drawn his.

"*Tenho fome, Capitão.*"

"He wants to eat," I told Doyle.

"*Christ!*" Doyle hissed, peering at his watch. "Can't he see it's three o'clock in the morning?"

After breakfast I had a confab with the Indian. Although my Portuguese was very limited I managed to learn his name—Manolo—and that he wished to offer his services as our guide. There was a village, he assured me, a few days distant.

Doyle, however, was not convinced that we should put ourselves in Manolo's hands. "What if it's a trick? What if there are more of them up ahead in this so-called village? And what about food? We've barely got enough for ourselves. And now we'll have to feed this motherfucker."

Over coffee we assessed our supplies. We had three pounds of flour, a pound of rice, two pounds of beans, half a pound of coffee, four cans of evaporated milk for our *café com leite*, some water purification tablets, sulfa and quinine, several bars of rapadur*a*, some dried apricots, a few boxes of raisins, two quarts of whiskey, and our money cache—3,000,000 *cruzeiros* and nine 100-dollar bills American.

Finally Doyle grudgingly agreed that our chances of surviving were better with Manolo than without him.

"I guess we'll just have to trust him. Do you think he's on the level? Can this guy actually get us to this village or whatever it is?"

As though he had grasped the import of Doyle's question, Manolo smiled faintly and muttered, "*Se Deus quize, Capitão...*"

During the days that followed it became increasingly apparent, as Doyle and I agreed, that our decision had been a fortunate one. Although we didn't seem to be getting any closer to the village our diet greatly improved. The forest was teeming with animals, fish and birds, and Manolo knew which ones to eat and how to get them. Wild turkeys, pigs and iguanas he furnished in abundance, as well as *veados*, a tiny forest deer, very wary, absolutely delicious, and more than once he came up with a clutch of turtle eggs which were wonderful hard-boiled, creamy and very filling. Our survival now seemed so assured that I for one stopped worrying about getting to the village and enjoyed our day-to-day existence to the hilt for the adventure of it and for the wonders we encountered on our way—a transparent glass frog whose skeleton and beating heart were clearly visible, a praying mantis that perfectly imitated a leaf, a large lizard that tried to elude us by mimicking not only the color but the texture of the forest floor (we ate him).

Manolo was an excellent companion, cheerful and considerate, more than willing to carry his portion of the load, always ready with our *café com leite* in the morning. It didn't seem to matter to him how many miles we made in a day or whether we were in fact "getting anywhere." Due to the lack of a common language I was able to learn very little of his background except that his home village was "far away" and that he had a wife and small children. Also, in the jungles of Brazil, one does not press men one meets on the trail for details of their personal lives. One of the first things I noticed about Manolo was that he squatted to urinate, like a woman. Later he informed me that a piranha had eaten his penis.

One day after Manolo had shot a monkey and we'd put away a delicious meal, Doyle said to me: "Ask him where we can get some girls. Anything! I don't care what they look like. Tell him we'll pay."

It was strange... Here were three men in a trackless jungle with only a handful of words between us—I didn't even know how to say "woman" in Portuguese—yet in seconds I was able to convey Doyle's request to Manolo. He grinned, then squatted and began scratching in the mud with a stick. Curiously, what he drew was not a map but rather something like an ideogram—houses, an airplane, and a crude human figure with pendulous breasts.

"I will take you to *Las Casas, Capitão.*"

After studying his stick drawing for a bit longer Manolo stood up, turned halfway around and pointed at the bush. And off we went, into the thickest stuff I've ever seen— massive trees linked by networks of strangling vines and rank undergrowth bristling with stinging nettles and punishing thorns. After an hour or so of this madness we reached a spot near a riverbank very much like the spot where Manolo had made his drawing—in fact, I would almost be willing to swear it was the same spot. Here, following Manolo's lead, we secured the guns in our packs, took off our boots and plunged into the shallow river. We were headed downstream now and with the current behind us we walked with loping, weightless steps. I felt elated. We were moving with the jungle now instead of fighting it.

As night began to fall Manolo led us out of the river. We walked a short distance through the bush—the trees had thinned out—then Manolo paused, apparently listening intently to a sound only he could hear. He smiled and nodded at us encouragingly, then we resumed walking. A little farther on, same performance. Again, I could hear nothing at all. We went on. A third pause. This time I heard it—music, very faint, but it was unmistakably music—with a samba beat. We continued on. Now we could see a glow of pulsing lights. There was a clearing up ahead in the jungle. The music was louder now. I saw barbed wire, a gate, and a guard with a gun.

"We have arrived, *Capitão*."

At the gate we got a shake from the guards. The man took Doyle's Ruger 357 and Manolo's 38 special. I wasn't carrying anything except my machete and a Buck knife but the guy took them too.

Once we were inside the dancehall the strangeness began to wear off. It was just like any whorehouse in Mexico except that the bouncers were packing guns and the girls—Indian maidens in halters and miniskirts—spoke Portuguese.

After a few *cerveja*s I selected a girl. She said her name was Daniela. The price was amazingly cheap. I think it was 2,400 cruzeiro*s*. The rooms were outside, in a courtyard. Chickens pecked in the red dust and a tapir sniffed at our toes as we made our way past the rows of stalls to our *cuarto*.

Back at the bar, I waited for Doyle to return, which he soon did, looking rumpled and flushed, and we ordered more cervejas.

At the bar we met Dr. Siquieros, who came from Madrid and spoke excellent Castilian but no English, a bright and articulate man with whom I sensed an immediate rapport. Dr. Siquieros filled me in on some of the background of "*Las Casas*," the jungle whorehouse. It was owned by an American, Charles W. Lockheed, a mechanical engineer who'd made a fortune developing some sort of a fitting for an oil-drilling bit and had come to South America to build an empire in the jungle and live out his fantasies. *Las Casas* was famous throughout Brazil, Dr. Siquieros explained, and although most of the patrons were gold miners, smugglers and bandeirantes, it was also popular with tourists, who called the place "Señor Lucky's." "Señor Lucky," he went on, was a corruption of "Señor Lockheed." That is, when "Lockheed" is pronounced by a Spanish or Portuguese speaker, it comes out, "Lucky."

It was strange, I reflected, with a glance at Doyle who stood at the bar listening vaguely to Dr. Siquieros (Doyle didn't understand Spanish) as he surveyed the lineup of Indian girls, strange, but wasn't it Doyle's dream exactly that Señor Lucky was living out? Señor Lucky had made a bundle and he had built an empire in the jungle, a fantasy kingdom in which he could orchestrate his experiences as he wished, without the nagging bit and bridle that society puts in a man's mouth. It was Doyle's dream exactly— except that Señor Lucky had already realized his dream.

The old man—he was now past seventy, Dr. Siquieros said—had been a football star at Syracuse University, and as a part of his recreational fantasy Señor Lucky retained at his estate at the other end of the compound a number of young Indian girls outfitted in actual Syracuse University cheerleaders' uniforms—orange-and-black sweaters, pleated skirts, bobby socks and white shoes with pom-poms.

"When the mood comes over him he takes the little cheerleaders into his bedroom—sometimes five or six, sometimes ten—even twelve—an entire squad! Señor Lucky is a man of—how do you say—prodigious appetites."

I asked Dr. Siquieros if it would not be possible for Doyle and myself to meet Señor Lucky.

"Of course! If you will excuse me for a bit I will see if I can arrange it. Once he learns that you are Americans he will undoubtedly invite you to stay on for at least a week or two."

After Doyle had gone to the room with another girl and returned I filled him in on my conversation with Dr. Siquieros. A few minutes later the jungle doctor came back and led us outside into the compound.

We walked past an airstrip where a small plane was tethered, past a large loamy garden, clusters of huts, a watering trough, and finally a spacious lawn replete with croquet posts and wickets. Up ahead was a swimming pool and Jacuzzi and beyond that a stately mansion built in the Antebellum style of the American South.

Señor Lucky received us in his study. Although Dr. Siquieros had informed me that his age was seventy nine, the lord of this jungle empire looked no more than fifty. A formidable man, large, dynamic, wearing an editor's green eyeshade, he sat at a drafting desk cluttered with ceramic pots filled with pens, pencils, erasers, X-acto knives and the like.

"Welcome," he said. "I don't get many Americans here."

There was a tapping at the door and a smashing Indian girl entered, wearing an orange-and-black sweater, a short pleated skirt and white bunny-puffs. We were served iced drinks, Planter's Punch. Then Señor Lucky led us on a tour of the place. Everywhere you looked you saw the cheerleaders, just as Dr. Siquieros had said, vacuuming, dusting, polishing, busying silently about the great house.

"You look like you've played a little ball," Señor Lucky said suddenly, clapping me on the shoulder as we paused on the verandah. His manner was disarmingly affable, like that of a big friendly bear. At the same time his keen blue eyes were carefully sizing me up. I could hear his breath hissing through his hairy nostrils as he pulled me in close to his ponderous body.

"Yes, sir! Fullback, University of Miami," I blurted out, and quickly changed the subject. I'd never played football a day in my life and didn't know a touchdown from a hockey puck.

Señor Lucky showed us his gym. It was posh. Mirrored walls, red carpets, state-of-the-art exercise machines and free weights. One of the cheerleaders who was polishing a mirror gave a little gasp as Doyle peeled off his shirt, revealing his segmented torso. Doyle and I hadn't touched a weight in months but we decided to hoist a few just to keep our hand in. The results were shocking. My bench press had dropped to 325 and Doyle struggled with 350. The jungle had done its work.

Using a set of straps, Señor Lucky did a few shoulder shrugs with a heavy bar he picked off a squat rack. Apparently he excelled at this movement, which works mainly the trapezius. I smelled the sour sweat from his armpits as he glowered at us, making insolent little clucking sounds in his throat. Neither Doyle nor I could touch the weight Señor Lucky had used, even with the straps, and notwithstanding the fact that the man was more than fifty years our senior.

It was right after this that Doyle collapsed—apparently a recurrence of the stomach problem he'd experienced in Brasilia, only this time it was accompanied by dizziness and a sudden, high fever.

"Better get him right to bed," Señor Lucky said. "This sort of thing happens in the jungle. It comes over you quickly. It's a good thing I have an excellent doctor on the premises. He's the chap who brought you to me, in fact. Dr. Siquieros. Unfortunately, he speaks no English. But perhaps you—"

"Yes, of course. I'll take care of it."

After we'd gotten Doyle settled in a room under the care of Dr. Siquieros, Señor Lucky showed me to my room. It was spacious, clean, and there was a real bed. I felt elated.

It was now quite late and I was exhausted. It had been an eventful day and the bed with its crisp clean sheets looked wonderfully inviting. I went to check on Doyle and learned from Dr. Siquieros that his fever had fallen and he was resting comfortably. Also that a room had been found for Manolo in the servants' quarters.

I'd just gotten undressed when there came a knock at the door. It was Señor Lucky, with three of the cheerleaders in tow, and insisting that I permit the trio to spend the night with me. He wouldn't take no for an answer. The girls were giggly, full of fun, and utterly without inhibitions. It was a delightful night and nothing could have been further from the notion of "sin."

The days that followed were among the happiest of my life. I had everything a man could want: excellent quarters, good food, good companionship and good conversation (I mean Dr. Siquieros), and the attentions of the sweet cheerleaders. The gymnasium and pool were of course at my disposal, and if I felt like a stroll along a jungle trail, Manolo was always ready to accompany me.

Doyle remained in bed under the care of Dr. Siquieros who drew numerous blood samples in an effort to determine just what sort of bug Doyle had in his system. I was happy to get away from Doyle for a while. Aside from lifting weights and now our concerted struggle to survive in the jungle we had no interests in common. I was even more pleased when Señor Lucky began visiting Doyle daily to discuss the standings of the college and professional football teams, a subject about which I knew nothing whatever.

It might be imagined that Señor Lucky's life as lord over his jungle fantasy kingdom was a continual round of pleasure but that was not so. His romps with the cheerleaders were reserved for special evenings. He liked having them around; he basked in the special erotic ambiance he had created for himself, and this ambiance acted as a spur to his work, which was far and away his foremost interest. Although the income from his patented inventions and the revenue from the bar and brothel were more than sufficient to maintain his baronial lifestyle, he continued to work at his drawing board. The tables in his study were stacked high with drawings and blueprints, and often when the great man was seated for dinner I noticed that he'd forgotten to remove his green eyeshade. Frequently during the course of the meal he made notes on the tablecloth at his elbow.

Life at the great house, or *fazenda*, as the servants called it, followed a measured and stately rhythm. We began the day at six a.m. with café com leite, after which Señor Lucky went directly to his study. I was free to order a sumptuous breakfast if I chose but more often I'd content myself with coffee and fresh *suco de maracujá*, passion fruit juice. At noon I'd join Señor Lucky for lunch or sometimes I'd eat with the servants. In the afternoon, before dinner, drinks were served on the verandah by the delightful cheerleaders—tall frosty glasses of a delicious concoction which earlier I referred to as Planter's Punch, but which, as I learned, was actually *caipirinha*, the national drink of Brazil, made from *cachaça*, a jungle rum, crushed whole limes and sugar poured over cracked ice. Dinner itself was a leisurely affair and featured a varied menu expertly prepared by Alfredo Alcides de Alcazar, a hotel chef from Manaus who was paid a handsome salary to stay on at the jungle kingdom. Alfredo's *matambre* (literally, "kills hunger"), made with marinated tapir instead of the traditional flank steak, was incomparable, as were the vegetables from Señor Lucky's garden—spinach, carrots, onions and zucchini. *Feijoa* was, of course, a standby, as was a fragrant *carne con frutas*, pork stewed with apricots, raisins, almonds, cinnamon and orange juice. Sometimes a *veado*, a diminutive forest deer such as Manolo had shot for us, was substituted for pork, with excellent results. On one occasion we were served tender barbecued slivers of some kind of meat (it may have been turtle) wrapped in manioc leaves, which numbed the tongue like cocaine.

After dinner I'd repair to the dancehall for a few *cervejas* and to continue my ongoing discussions with Dr. Siquieros. As I said earlier, Dr. Siquieros and I hit it off very well. Doyle, on the other hand, didn't like Dr. Siquieros, mainly because the jungle doctor failed to measure up to Doyle's rigid standards of ultra-masculinity, his special all-American brand of barbershop machismo. Doyle referred to Dr. Siquieros as "the Queer" and "the Fruit," or "*El Maricón,*" the only word of Spanish Doyle knew. While Dr. Siquieros may have been, at least in appearance, a little swishy—he was slightly built with long eyelashes and a soft, drooping mustache—he had something Doyle never dreamed of having: a bright, inquisitive and expansive mind.

Was Dr. Siquieros even a "real" doctor, that is, a medical doctor? I couldn't be sure. In Brazil every man who considers himself of any consequence at all bears the title of Doctor or Colonel. The man himself was vague about his status as well as about his reasons for being in the jungle. I didn't press him for details. He didn't appear to be a dangerous man, but in Brazil one can never tell. Although he spoke no English he seemed to know London fairly well, also New York and LA. He mentioned that he'd taught Spanish Literature at the University of Madrid, and I believed him because it seemed to fit his character. The best thing about Dr. Siquieros, as far as I was concerned, was that he seemed to have plenty of time for conversation, and that he apparently felt, as I did, that our discussions and the ideas we tossed around were at least as important as whatever it was we had come to the jungle to do.

Dr. Siquieros's favorite topic for discussion was Señor Lucky—not in the sense of exchanging gossip about the man but rather Señor Lucky as a convenient and readily accessible archetype of the extraordinary man, an in-house model of the man of destiny.

"The man has 115 children," Dr. Siquieros told me one afternoon as we sat at our customary table in the dancehall with two saucy young Indian strumpets. "In these villages they call such children '*botos*,' that is, children sired by river dolphins. Señor Lucky treats his Indians well. He is kind, but stern, like a good father. They look up to him as their leader, almost as a god. As I may have already told you, his privileges among them include the *jus primus noctis*. And this privilege is freely given. Señor Lucky is not troubled, you see, by the great ennui such as you Americans complain of. This is a self-determined man. He makes his own rules. And his rules are fair and just. He is a benevolent despot. Which, by the way, is the best form of government. But today we no longer believe in the divine right of kings. The world has been stripped of myth…"

The next day Dr. Siquieros came to me with some grave news. Doyle's condition had worsened during the night.

"We must get your friend to a hospital. I can do no more for him here."

"What about the plane?"

"The plane. That is an interesting story. The plane is missing a part. Señor Lucky sent to Manaus for the part but they wrote back and said they had to send to São Paulo. They said it would take two months and already it has been three. That is the jungle."

Señor Lucky provided me with a company of six bearers who took turns carrying Doyle's litter, also with ample supplies of food and water for the journey to Iquitos, the nearest town of any size. With Manolo as our guide we started out through the jungle. I tried to share the burden of carrying Doyle, but since I was nearly a foot taller than the other men it was impossible. We made frequent stops to check Doyle's IV-bottle, which we kept suspended above his body lashed to a stick, and to make sure that the ropes with which we had secured him to the litter weren't cutting off his circulation at any point. Doyle slept most of the time. When he did wake up he was delirious and seemed to have no grasp of the situation.

And so we proceeded, a forced march through the jungle, with the tiny Indians bearing the litter of the great white god who had come to plunder the earth of its diamonds and gold. Manolo led, and sometimes I walked in front with him, or again sometimes I would drop back to the rear of the caravan. The men needed no encouragement or supervision. They marched bravely and seemed entirely cognizant of the seriousness of their task.

The march was uneventful until, on the morning of the third day, as we approached the confluence of the Ucayali and an unnamed river near Pucallpa and the trees thinned, I dropped back a considerable distance—I could see the entire party, which had halted—and Manolo also dropped back, and approached me solemnly.

"*Capitão*..."

"*Qué cosa, mi hijo?*"

"*Ele esta morto, Capitão.*"

Manolo and I walked slowly back to join the others. I was stunned. Ragged black *urubus*—vultures—were slowly circling, and green bottle flies had already laid eggs in the corners of Doyle's mouth. Doyle's death was *incidental*. There was nothing violent or dramatic about it. A single leaf had fallen from a tree and had become a part—not of death—but of the swarming, teeming life of the jungle, the life that is a fever, an infection, a contagion.

I ordered the stretcher-bearers to dig and we buried Doyle there on the muddy *praia* of the Ucayali River. I recited "*De La Muerte Oscura*," by Federico Garcia Lorca in Spanish and the *Lord's Prayer* in English, then we all stood for a few moments in silence around the grave.

It was decided that the six bearers would go back to Las Casas and Manolo and I would continue on to Iquitos. Accordingly, we divided up the food supplies and parted.

When we neared Iquitos I asked Manolo if he would care to stay in town for a few days at the Hotel Imperial Amazonas, as my guest. But he declined. Perhaps Manolo really was a fugitive, as Doyle and I had often conjectured, a murderer who wanders the forest making a living where he can, always afraid of being recognized. Or it may have been simply that he didn't feel comfortable anywhere except in the jungle.

I gave Manolo my portion of the food, my machete, my Buck knife, and also Doyle's Ruger 357 which I'd been carrying since we left Las Casas. Then I handed him a lump of bills, 850,000 cruzeiros. He stuffed the wad of bills into his pocket without counting it. I shook his hand, then we embraced.

"Goodbye, my friend. *Muito obrigado*."

Manolo's eyes filled with tears. "Go with God, Capitão."

In end-of-the-world Iquitos, a backwater town of washed-out gold miners, smugglers, mercenary soldiers and out-of-work riverboat captains, I sat at the bar of the Hotel Imperial Amazonas and felt for the first time in my life that famous ennui which soldiers sometimes experience after a war. Up until now I had been carried along by the stream of events. I'd been towed in a drunken boat by a giant fish down a legendary river into the very heart of darkness. As I looked back over it now, the hardships we'd endured—the hunger, the stinging insects, the parasites that burrow under the skin—all that somehow fell away, leaving only the high spots, as if it had all been a grand adventure, the shimmering panorama that opened before the prow of the *bataloa*, the comradeship of brave, uncomplaining men, the empire in the center of the jungle and the white man who transformed himself into a god.

In the jungle there had been no time to reflect, to question, to be afraid. Whatever of fear I experienced was momentary, born of an instant. The night, for example, when I stepped out of the savoropanco on the praia of the Rio Branco and heard a jaguar cough, very near; the moment when I awoke in the blue grotto and saw Manolo, armed to the teeth. But now I felt a dull, oppressive, indefinable fear, the neurotic fear that paralyzes a man and makes him incapable of acting, incapable of living. I was not only bored, I was *scared*. If the jungle could kill a big strapping man like Doyle Junghammer it could kill me, too.

Days went by. I didn't know what to do. I wanted to be out in the bush, hungry, exhausted, wet, uncertain, but *alive*. But the struggle to survive was over. I had won. It should have been a time of celebration. But under the circumstances... Dimly I realized that I was obligated to contact Doyle Junghammer's wife, to inform her that I had buried her husband in an unmarked grave at the confluence of the Rio Ucayali and an unknown river near Pucallpa in the wilds of South America.

More days passed and I did nothing. I counted my money. I had two 100-dollar bills American, 300,000 *cruzeiros* and some chickenfeed—just enough for a plane ticket, as it turned out. A plane... Yes, of course. It was becoming clear to me now. I had to catch a plane. I had to get   out   of   Iquitos...

9

New York, New York! More dreary, weary, drunken days with Hal Feldman. *Top of the heap? King of the hill?* I was out of rabbits and out of hats. I suppose I could have gotten a job picking fly shit out of pepper. But then I got a call from Roddy Joplin in Clear Lake. He was back from Mexico and he'd married again. His sixth? Seventh? A librarian this time, and he'd quit his trucking job and was now driving the Bookmobile at the Mason City Library. Consequently his old boss, Chubby Thorwaldsson, needed a driver to fill Roddy's spot, and come on in, the water's fine.

I suspected that Roddy's offer of help was not entirely altruistic, that his newest marriage was already crumbling, that he'd soon be running again for Thorwaldsson, and that he envisioned the two of us on the road together, batting ideas back and forth like ping pong balls as we crossed the continent on eighteen wheels.

Nevertheless, I badly needed to make some money and I resolved to seize this opportunity, which now appeared to me to be my ticket to a new life.

Now that everything was decided, I had to act quickly. To delay would mean to sink down once again into the quagmire of the day-to-day insanity with Hal. I had to extricate myself. I had to get to Clear Lake, pronto,

I decided to call my parents in Cooperstown to see if I could squeeze the bus fare out of them. *Typical Jerzy*, I thought, as I dialed the operator. *Not a word for over a year and now he calls collect asking for money. Collect, mind you, he calls! That's the worst of it. Where did we go wrong?*

The upshot of it was that my father wired me fifty dollars, and I learned during the course of the brief, uneasy conversation that my sister Erin had become engaged to one Fosley Brandt, and that their wedding was coming up in late August.

On the night before my departure for Iowa, I got back to the centipede's nest on Sullivan and heard a commotion in the bathroom, Hal with one of his girls. Nothing unusual, he had a million of them. As I was rummaging around in the refrigerator, Hal emerged from the bathroom in his boxer shorts and greeted me.

"Hey, Jerzy! Am I glad to see you! It's that girl from the bar. You'll recognize her when you see her. She's the one with the yellow cat. Hey, by the way, we got the job on Prince Street. We'll use the leftover paint from the Charles Street job. Oh, shit, I forgot. You're splitting! But listen. This Yellow Cat Girl. Do you want to have a go at her? I've got her primed up pretty good. A little play on words there! *Get it? Leftover paint? Primed up?* Not bad, eh? The old maestro's got it goin' on!"

"Yeah, you're the Man, Hal. No question about that."

"But seriously, do you want to take her off my hands? I didn't realize she had a game leg. I can't deal with a thing like that. It's…it's…I don't know. I mean, shit, it probably wouldn't make any difference to a guy like you, but me, I'm kinda, well…*persnickety*. I mean, Christ Almighty, I got her legs up in the air and then I saw that special shoe! Those things are *eerie!* My dick retracted like a fried noodle! I think she's a little ditzy, too. Loco in the coco. She started crying and shit. Great tits, though! But I just can't hack it. She's all yours, bro. Be a pal, will you?"

Hal left and I joined the Yellow Cat Girl in the bathroom and got her calmed down. And I did recognize her from the bar: *Brenda! Blonde, halfway pretty Brenda Boudreau. Vodka martini, three olives!*

It just goes to show you: the sun even shines on a dog's ass once in a while.

I asked Brenda if she wanted me to walk her home.

"No, I'm going back to the bar."

"Fine! I'll go with you."

At the bar I ordered a beer for myself and a drink for Brenda.

"My God, Jerzy! Vodka martini, three olives! How did you know that?"

"Lucky guess!"

"Hal's very…abrupt, isn't he? He's moody, I guess. I think he's a genius. In fact, I'm sure he's a genius. I know he's a great writer. But he's so self-centered. He's very self-centered. But he's also very sensitive—"

"Jesus! Do we have to talk about *him?*"

"What would you rather talk about?"

"You!"

"Me? Not worth talking about. You don't want to get mixed up with me. I'm clinically depressed. I'm an alcoholic, a real lowlife."

"What do you think, I live at the Ritz?"

I spent the night on Brenda's couch with her yellow cat, after we'd polished off a half-gallon jug of Mona Lisa Tokay. Nothing much happened, at least as far as I can remember, but there were some goodbye kisses in the morning, and I promised to send her a postcard from Clear Lake.

Back at Sullivan Street I got my Mercury Movers winged-foot baseball cap out of my gym bag and put it on. Time to fly the coop! Earlier on I'd performed a nifty bit of battlefield surgery on my screenplay, which had been cut to ribbons by the rapier thrusts of the swashbuckling Russian director Sergey Billetnikov, and now the thing was starting to write itself. I stashed the script in a drawer and it was as if I were tucking my characters in for a nap, or putting my wooden soldiers away in their barracks for a while. Awake or asleep, my wooden soldiers were marching in formation, storming the barricades, fraternizing with the enemy, even. I felt elated. My doubts had vanished, doubts about my screenplay, and doubts about going to Clear Lake, as well.

It went off like clockwork—the trip to Clear Lake by bus, the meeting with Roddy Joplin, and my new digs, a rented room in the home of a good prairie mother. Roddy took a day off from the bookmobile and we pulled a load of corn up to the grain elevators at Savage, Minnesota, about a hundred miles. It was just like the old days and yet it wasn't, because Roddy had shed his cowboy duds. He was dressed like an ordinary citizen, Levis, plaid shirt, Nike shoes. After I'd parked Chubby Thorvaldsson's rig in the company yard back at Clear Lake we walked to Roddy's car and he got a pint of Old Cabin Still out of the glove compartment.

"Sure, I know I'm drinking too much. Wasn't it Winston Churchill who said you can't make a good speech on ice water? Shit, look at Hemingway, Fitzgerald, Faulkner. I mean, look at Faulkner! Could Joyce have written *Finnegan's Wake* if he wasn't drinking? We'll never know, because James Joyce never drew a sober breath in his life!"

We went by the house so I could meet Roddy's new wife, Maryann, the librarian. We sat in the living room with our beers, Maryann on the couch and Roddy next to her. Maryann was a male woman, a *marimacho*. In the first few moments it became clear that she disapproved of me and the edgy Gypsy lifestyle, which in her mind, presumably, I represented. Roddy had told her that I was a writer, and it seemed ironic to me that a librarian should be so dead set against a writer.

I noticed that Roddy had taken to smoking a pipe. His

manner seemed rather patronizing. He'd made the great leap, from the blue-collar world to academia, whereas I was still wallowing around in the pig-muck, snouting up the odd rutabaga. Would I ever be a *real* writer? He gave me a sidelong glance, narrowing his eyes, cradling the pipe. *How's the work going?* This, as if he were talking about a ruptured appendix.

Roddy was sitting next to Maryann, but somehow he appeared to be sitting on her lap. Roddy was her little man-thing, a nebbish she kept in the vest pocket of her Marcy Allen suit. That was clear as a bell. The tension in the room was terrific. We swilled our beers down and Roddy poured everybody a snifter of Jim Beam. Maryann had done a hitch in the Marines, I learned. A regular drill sergeant, John Wayne with tits.

Chubby Thorvaldsson put me in an old International "highbinder" with a 12-speed Spicer transmission. You had to split every gear. I started running from Clear Lake up to the grain elevators at Savage. I made two trips a day loaded with corn. There were days, however, when I made only one trip because I'd dreamed off at the wheel and missed my stop and ended up in Minneapolis. This happened quite frequently. There was a big parking lot near a Tastee Freez where I'd make a U-turn.

The thing was, I was used to running long miles, I mean pulling for Schneider. Barstow to Baton Rouge, Memphis to Tacoma. This milk run of Chubby's just wasn't something I could cotton to. I couldn't take the monotony of it. And then there's the unending *flatness* of Iowa. You wouldn't think that wide open spaces could be a prison, but it's true. Or maybe it's the way the corn whispers at night. A month went by, then two, and I began to wish that I'd set sail for Belize in a concrete boat. I was going batty. *Anywhere out of this flatness!* I even thought about calling up Reggie Ray to see if he had a spot for me. I figured I could run with Armando again—even with M'butu from Mogadishu. Anything but this…

There was a little diner about halfway to Savage from Clear Lake. I can't remember the name. They had a wonderful creation called a Bird's Nest Burger. It was soupy ground beef in barbecue sauce on a Kaiser roll, topped with Parmesan cheese. One day at the diner I met a woman named Lula who said she was looking for a driver to move her carnival—Tallulah's All-American Road Show—from town to town. She'd put me in a new Kenworth conventional with a condo sleeper and we'd be running more or less forty-eight states. I saw my chance to get out of the rut I was in, running that old highbinder up to Savage every day, so I said yes.

I thought Roddy would be pissed but he was very understanding about the whole thing. Besides, he had Maryann to contend with.

I gave Chubby Thorvaldsson my notice and helped to tear down the carnival. I worked with Bucky Blankenship from Bogalusa, Louisiana. Bucky's dream was to hook up with Lash LaRue, the once famous cowboy actor who was now on the skids and playing fairs and carnivals with his King of the Bullwhip act. Bucky had been chasing Lash all over the country.

"1 know we'll catch up with Lash someday," Bucky said. "He's only a few towns ahead of us now. And when we do, when we do catch up with Lash, everything is gonna be *different*."

Our supervisor was Eric, Lula's son-in-law. Eric was the boss when the show was on the road. We got everything loaded on the trucks and we went up to Faribault, then over to Fargo and Billings and Boise. Right away, before we left Faribault, Lula asked me if I wanted to make some extra money by working as outside talker for her monkey show, the Savage Ape Family. I said yes.

"The Savage Ape Family! Giant apes from the jungles of Borneo! They will both astound and amuse you! Giant apes, ladies and gentlemen... You'll meet them on the inside! They *are* alive... Giant apes from the jungles of

Borneo… Savage apes! They *are* alive!"

My job was to rap off this shtick over and over and try to get people into the joint. I had a tape I could play of the same thing, which was how I learned it. But I was only allowed to play the tape on breaks because Lula wanted a live person up there, talking.

When the strippers saw I was pretty good with the bally they asked me to announce their act, or rather they asked Lula if she could spare me part of the time. The strippers had a tape, but star stripper Electra, Lula's daughter, insisted that if Lula's Savage Ape Family rated an outside talker, then surely the strippers deserved one too. So I started announcing Electra. How could I say no?

"Electra! The Electrifying Enchantress from New Orleans, Land of Dreams. A little treat from the Land of Jean Lafitte! She will both electrify and excite you! One million volts of pure electricity! She jiggles, she wiggles, she does the hoochie-koochie! You'll see it all…on the inside. The exciting, the enchanting, the electrifying—Electra!"

A week later I began announcing Melissa Montague, the Mississippi Little Darlin', who had recently come to us from Big John Strong's Circus.

"Melissa Montague, Mis-sus-sippi Little Darlin'! She takes it all off, on the inside! Right down to the bare essentials, folks, right down to the bare essentials. She gets down and dirty! The pretty little princess from Pascagoula! Mis-sus-sippi Little Darlin', Melissa Montague! She takes it all off…on the inside!"

Bucky and I consulted Billboard Magazine religiously for listings of Lash LaRue's performances with different fairs and carnivals in various towns and cities, and Bucky continued to go on and on about Lash.

"When we catch up with Lash, maybe in Baton Rouge, maybe in Charleston, we'll get on with his show. He's still got his Wild West Act and he cracks the bullwhip. Oh, it's nothin' like the film days, but he's still holdin' his head up. He's still Lash LaRue. We'll get our own trailers, I guarantee it. I know Lash. He'll set us up proper."

Bucky needed his daily fix of hope. He needed to believe that he'd one day hook up with Lash LaRue and that his life would change dramatically, just like those so-called Savage Apes needed to believe that they'd someday get back to the jungles of Borneo or Africa or wherever.

Nearly everyone in the carnival was family except Bucky Blankenship and myself. Eric was Electra's husband, and Electra was Lula's daughter, and so on. Lula, a retired stripper, did the hiring and firing and all the booking, bookkeeping and accounting. Eric was the straw boss, and he was also working on a knife-throwing act. Every day he practiced with the knives, using his wife Electra as a target. He was very good.

Eric was an alpha male, the jealous type. His relationship with Electra was extremely volatile. They were always at each other's throats. And now that I was working the strip show, Eric began to get the idea that I was fooling around with Electra, which wasn't at all true. He asked me if I wanted to give it a try, standing up against a wall while he threw the knives. I declined.

Eric the Knife thought the rest of us existed only to compete for the privilege of kissing his ass. He paraded around like a little John Gotti. Eric was a Dale Carnegie aficionado, a be-all-you-can-be nut. He carried the book around with him, the Dale Carnegie book, *How to Win Friends and Influence People*. His one idea was to take it to the max. Eric's dream was to get his knife-throwing act on prime time TV, with Circus Vargas and Big John Strong's Circus as stepping stones.

Right behind Eric at every moment was Dickie the midget, trotting after his idol on his stumpy legs. Dickie was a roustabout. He did odd jobs. He lifted weights, too. I used to spot him, hand him his bench presses. The kid really busted his ass, supersets, forced reps, you name it. Dickie was buffed, no question about it, but as Electra remarked one day, "No matter how much Dickie works out, all he's ever gonna be is a *muscular midget*."

Eric had a tiny TV in his trailer and the two of them, Eric and Dickie, spent a lot of time drinking beer and watching a Dale Carnegie human potential program. Eric had memorized some of the patter, and he'd spiel it off at odd moments, like when Dickie and Bucky and I were helping him set up in a new town.

"In 1838, he ran for speaker of the State legislature. He lost. In 1843, he ran for Congress. He lost. Are you listening, Dickie?"

"Right, Mister Eric."

"In 1854, he ran for the Senate. He lost. In 1856, he sought the vice presidential nomination at his party's national convention. He got less than a hundred votes. *Dickie?*"

"I'm listening, Mister Eric."

"In 1858, he ran for the Senate again. Again he lost. Then, in 1860, he was elected President of the United States. That man was—*Dickie?*"

"Abraham Lincoln, Mister Eric."

"That's right, Dickie. Abraham Lincoln. You got it, Dickie?"

"I got it, Mister Eric."

"You say you got it, but have you *got* it? *If you can dream it, you can do it*. Dale Carnegie. You gotta think big, Dickie! Chuck Norris is a Dale Carnegie graduate, you know."

"Chuck Norris. *Way of the Dragon!*"

"That's right, Chuck Norris, *Way of the Dragon*, that's right. Wake up and smell the coffee, Dickie. You better get your shit together, boy. Never underestimate the power of the imagination. We gotta think big, Dickie. We gotta dream big, and then we gotta make it happen. If you can dream it, you can do it! Let me hear you say it, Dickie."

"If...you can dream it...you can do it."

"Louder! Say it like you mean it!"

"*If you can dream it, you can do it!*"

Dickie was eating it up, all right. When Eric talked that

shit Dickie's eyes sparkled with lust and you could see the desperate bravado of his sweaty schoolboy dreams blossoming behind his retinas, dreams he'd hoarded for years, the same way old men save useless balls of string in tortured rooms. *Image, stardom, tailfins! The dewy bodies of women!*

"By the way, we gotta see that movie again. Write that down, will you? *You don't got a pencil?* Jesus Christ, Dickie! Here, take this one. Okay, write that down, about *Way of the Dragon.* Okay? Okay? We gotta start writing things down."

Actually, Dickie the midget was the only person Eric was at all nice to. He'd spot Dickie when he did his squats and hand him his bench presses, and that sort of thing. He even gave his little butt monkey a copy of the Dale Carnegie Book, *How to Win Friends and Influence People,* with an inscription, "*Think big, Dickie! Eric the Knife.*"

When we got over to Boise, Eric the Knife and Electra had a huge blowout. It didn't have anything to do with me, thank God. Eric had accused Electra of turning a trick with a mark and he'd threatened to kill her. Lula called me into her trailer and told me that Electra would be sleeping in the Kenworth until things blew over and I'd have to sleep in the joint with her monkey act, the Savage Ape Family.

The so-called Savage Apes, Samson and Delilah and their son, Dizzy, were either big chimpanzees or small gorillas. And they were either feeble or feeble-minded or both—and they were anything but savage. They were mangy and moth-eaten, completely docile and understandably neurotic.

It was close quarters in the trailer, I can tell you. My lumpy single bunk was only a few feet away from the apes' cage. The animal stink of those apes made my eyes water. But it wasn't so much the stink of them that I couldn't stand. It was their scratching. They were awake all night, scratching, moaning, whimpering and rattling the bars of their cage. You heard them scratching and scratching, and then one of them would catch a louse and crack it open and eat it. Then back to more scratching and moaning. They seemed to have the weight of the world on their shoulders. I guess they just wanted to get out of their cage and get back to the jungle.

And then I started getting them. I'm talking now about fleas. Not lice, but fleas! I woke up one night and my bunk was hopping with fleas. Those fleas had left those scrawny apes behind and they'd discovered a new continent, a new land overflowing with milk and honey. What a bonanza! A muscular young man, corn-fed, milk-fed marbled prime beef, with good old Type 0 blood and plenty of it! *Thank you, Jesus!* Those adventurous and intrepid fleas had themselves a field day until we got down to Cheyenne and I managed to sneak into town to get some insecticide. It was awful stuff and had almost as much of a stink to it as those apes, but it did the trick.

Lula liked to get lushed up on So-Co, Southern Comfort. She'd invite me to her trailer to talk. We'd sit at the kitchen table, and Lula's feeble little Chihuahua, Margo, would be curled up asleep at her feet.

"You come on down to Gal-*ves*-ton, Honey. Lula'll show you a good time. Oh, I got a few miles on me, Honey, but you know you can't play a pretty tune on a fiddle till it's broke in real good. By the way, you sound just fine out there. I was gonna have Eric do the bally for Electra, but you see, Eric can't stand the way the marks look at Electra. He can't be around that. He'll go fuckin' crazy. He really will. Oh, look how Margo's sleepin' so nice. Don't she look just like an angel?"

It was eerie sometimes when the little angel would wake up. She'd get to her feet and stand there, trembling all over. She was making a tremendous effort just to exist, every muscle tense and quivering. It gave you the creeps to look at her, with her pinched face and that sorrowful look in her enormous brown eyes, eyes that looked as if they'd been peeled with a flensing knife. Slap a pair of black wings on her and she'd pass for a fruit bat.

"Yeah, I remember one time we come into Hays City and the cottonwoods was all in bloom. We got set up and I was dancin' real good. God, they was throwin' me quarters and dollars and even five spots. Oh, boy, Sweetie, they loved me in Hays City!"

I'd take the dog outside to pee and Lula would freshen up our drinks.

"I'm old enough to be your mama, honey. That's why I'm gonna send you home. Oh, but don't go yet, darlin'. Have one more drink. Tell me honestly, do you think I'm attractive? Tell me the truth, honey. Darlin', I been over the road. I know it shows in my face. *Do you think I'm attractive?* Be honest, please. Honey, I done the best I could in my life and it's been a hard road to travel. But I will say one thing: *They loved me in Hays City!* Well, have one more drink, honey. I ain't gonna touch you. Don't worry about that. Just keep me company for a little while. God, the nights are so long…"

We went the round of the towns, Salt Lake, Provo, Grand Junction, Wichita. Electra and Eric made up and I went back to my sleeper berth in the Kenworth. At Oke City we turned and headed west, and just over the Texas border on I-40 I got separated from the caravan. A big wind came up and started pushing my trailer all over the road. I pulled into a rest stop near Shamrock and talked with a Werner driver who said he'd pulled off for the same reason. He said the wind was going to get bigger. He asked me how much I had on and I said, thirty-four thousand. He said, don't even think about getting back out there. I've got fifty-five and I'm shutting down.

I was a day and a night at that rest stop. There was the candy machine and the soft drink machine and the coffee machine and that was it. I had time to think, to take stock of my life, and as usual nothing added up. I'd gone to New York to become a writer and I'd ended up driving a truck out of Clear Lake, Iowa. And now I was touring forty-eight states with Tallulah's All-American Road Show. For all the sense any of it made I might as well have spent the last two years playing Chinese badminton.

Alienation, dehumanization, deracination… The good old Roddy Joplin Outsider's Index. I didn't need anybody to pull my chart to confirm that I was progressing quite nicely. Finally the wind died down and I hauled ass. I caught up with the show in Amarillo.

The weeks went by and the towns went by, Albuquerque, Gallup, Holbrook, Flagstaff. I kept hanging out with Bucky Blankenship after hours. We'd go to Mae's on the midway for beers after Bucky closed his ring toss booth and then we'd sit on the deserted merry-go-round horses and get sloshed and talk. One night we were at our usual station on the silent carrousel, sitting on our motionless wooden horses, and Bucky started in once again with the Lash LaRue stuff, which was beginning to wear a bit thin with me.

"Listen, forget about that shit," I said. "The hell with Lash LaRue! Sure, maybe he wowed the girls once with his cowboy looks and his blacksnake whip, but you've been over the road. You've seen the worst of it. Lash is nothing but one of those cardboard cutouts they set up in front of a movie matinee. You'd make three of him! Let's forget that shit and concentrate on our own business. Think about yourself, brother."

But the next day I got to thinking that I'd been pretty high handed in trying to wean Bucky away from his dreams, so I agreed to write a letter to Lash for Bucky, and we'd send it in care of Billboard Magazine. Maybe Bucky's scheme wasn't so crazy after all, because although Lash LaRue had a reputation for hard living—ten marriages, several drug busts and a lifelong bout with the bottle—I'd also heard many times that Lash LaRue was a man of generous sentiments. Sure, I admit, it was a long shot, but for Bucky just about everything was a long shot. This letter to Lash LaRue was pretty much Bucky's last chance to grab the brass ring.

Bucky dictated and I wrote:

Dear Mr. LaRue, I don't expect you'll remember me, but my name is Bucky Blankenship from Bogalusa, Louisiana, and I met you when we was both working the Ohio State Fair back around three years ago. You gave me a autographed photo of yourself, Lash LaRue, King of the Bullwhip, and you said you might could find some work for me one day being as how we was both from Louisiana and all. I been on the road for ten years now and I am experienced in all phases of carnival work. I would be much obliged if you could find a spot for me, Mr. LaRue. I have seen many of your films and I like 'Lonesome Cowboy' best of all.

Your sincere friend and admirer,
Bucky Blankenship

When we landed in Long Beach, Bucky and I got away from the carnival and went to a dance in Lakewood where we met Mildred, a girl Bucky knew from the last time the show had passed through town. Mildred worked in a paper box factory. Her hands were red and rough and covered with paper cuts, but she had great tits. I danced with her and got pretty crazed. Then we danced a second time and she threw her arms around me. She kissed me again and again. I knew she was spoken for but she didn't seem to care. But Bucky was my buddy so I just got the hell out of there.

When we hit Fresno, Bucky and I took another night off. We went to Mae's on the midway for the sausage sandwich and we drank some beers. Then we got on the Ferris wheel. We didn't have to pay, of course. Bucky had a bottle of Ancient Age. He was sloshed and in a desperate mood.

"God, I wish I'd stayed back there in Lakewood with Mildred. I could have been married by now and workin' at the factory. Jesus, you look down on everything from up here and what do you see? A goddamn frog pond. Some bitch spits out her eggs in the dirty water and here comes a joker and he pisses on her ovaries, and you got you a million damn tadpoles! Pollywogs! A million fuckin' people tryin' to get in the door! You got you a Chinaman's chance in this world, brother. This whole damn world is a fuckin' carnival. We're the marks, bro! Don't you see that? We're the marks!"

Bucky had a crush on Electra, Lula's daughter, Electra the Electrifying Enchantress. But he was treading on dangerous ground and he knew it, because Electra belonged to Eric the Knife. Electra was always showing up with a black eye or two and her arms covered with bruises, and we all knew that Eric regularly beat the shit out of her.

We'd get together at Lula's trailer, nights after the show closed, or in the mornings sometimes for breakfast, Lula, Electra, Bucky and I, and sometimes Melissa Montague, the Mississippi Little Darlin'. We'd all sit at the kitchen table and talk. Every time we got together it was the same thing, I mean the conversations between Lula and Electra.

"You can't leave the show, Pumpkin. Where would you go? What would you do?"

"I don't know, Mama. I don't know."

"I will say one thing for Eric, honey, and it's the only good thing I can say about him: he is ambitious. He wants to be somebody, and I really do believe that one of these days he's gonna make it."

"But that's just it, Mama. I don't want to be somebody. I just want to be a regular person." Electra would get up and pace the floor. "A regular person! Can you understand that, Mama? I don't want to be somebody. I want to be a nobody. The marks got it better than we do, Mama, the regular people. Is it so bad being a regular person? They got a home and a yard and kids. And a dog."

"I got a dog."

"Oh, Jesus, Mama! That's not what I mean. They got a place where they belong in the world. That's what I want. I want to be like the marks. I want to be a real person."

Melissa wanted out too. She wanted to get away from the carnival. Sometimes after closing Melissa and I would sit on the carousel horses and share a 40-ounce King Cobra. Or more often the Mississippi Little Darlin' would sit on a motionless white charger and I'd stand at her side, like a groom attending the horse of a princess, and she'd talk about going back home.

"Ottumwa! You're not from Pascagoula?"

"Hell no. Ottumwa. Ottumwa, Iowa."

"Ottumwa. The prairie stretches out forever and the corn whispers at night."

"You got it."

"My God, why would you want to go back?"

"Ottumwa? A lot of reasons. The road gets old after a while. All them men grabbin' at ya. Back in Ottumwa I was studying to be a veterinary technician. Then I won that stupid Miss Squash Blossom contest. I rode on a float in the homecoming parade and I thought I was on my way to Graceland. Then Big John Strong's Circus came to town, and when he left, I left! But now I want to go back. I want to go back to school. I always loved animals. Fact is, I like animals better than people. Oh, I'll miss the carnival, sure, in a way, I'll miss it. The bally gets in your blood."

Why did I hang out with Melissa? She was good company and sure, I thought maybe I could sample her wares, but more than that, even though I knew it was crazy, I was starting to fall for the Mississippi Little Darlin'.

One day Electra and Melissa took some time off and drove the bumper cars. In shorts and halters, without their hard glittery stripper personas, they were having fun like ordinary young girls. Bucky and I were sitting with coffees at Mae's, and Bucky jumped up, hopped into a bumper car and took off after Electra. Melissa, suddenly serious, crashed into Bucky's rig and pushed him off to the side, and Electra let out a joyful yelp.

"Yeah, Melissa! Way to go!"

The girls went on with their rollicking fun, and Bucky, sunk in gloom, tootled around by himself.

When Lula went grocery shopping, Bucky and I always went along to help carry the groceries and just to get away from the carnival for a while. But our trips to the supermarket were anything but pleasant because our driver was Eric the Knife.

One Friday we all piled into Lula's battered old Cadillac. Lula sat in the passenger seat with little Margo snoozing on her lap. Bucky and I were in the back seat. Electra, sitting between us, was dozing.

Huge raindrops began striking the windshield. Lula took a pull on her bottle of So-Co. "Looks like rain."

Eric, behind the wheel, maintained a stony silence.

"I said...it looks like rain."

No answer from Eric.

"Well, fuck you, then!"

"Mama, I'm tryin' to sleep back here."

"Well, ex-*cuse* me all to hell! You two... Jesus Christ! You know, it burns my ass. You think you got the world by the tail just because you're young. You'll find out..."

"Please, Mama..."

Lula fiercely hugged the sleeping dog. "At least you still love me, dontcha, Pumpkin?" She gulped down another slug of So-Co.

The rain became a torrent. Visibility was nil. Electra was getting nervous. "Eric, ain't you gonna turn on the windshield wipers?"

Eric didn't switch on the wipers and he didn't answer either. A sly smile crept across his handsome mug. He was enjoying Electra's discomfort.

"I wasn't always old, you know."

"We never said you was, Mama."

"I'll tell you one thing. They loved me in Hays City."

"Eric, turn on the fucking windshield wipers!"

"Shut up!"

"Eric!"

"Shut the fuck up!"

The rain was coming down in sheets. We couldn't see a damn thing. I was scared, and I could tell that Bucky was scared too. But we didn't dare say anything. Not with Eric the Knife at the wheel.

Electra was beside herself. "Jesus Christ, Eric!"

Eric turned on the wipers just in time to hit the brakes and avoid running up on a pickup truck in front of us. The Cadillac fishtailed but Eric quickly regained control and continued to pilot the car in sullen silence. He was probably wishing we'd crashed into the pickup.

Margo woke up and began whining softly.

"She's gotta piss, Eric. The dog's gotta piss."

Eric drove on in silence.

"Eric, the dog's gotta piss. Eric—"

"Shut...the fuck...up! Can you do that? Can you? Jesus Christ! Goddamn you, shut up! Shut up! Shut up! Shut the fuck up!"

When we arrived at the supermarket it was a huge relief to get away from Eric. He waited in the car. Same deal at the 99 Cent Store. We'd always stop by the 99 Cent Store after the supermarket.

At the 99 Cent Store, Lula loaded up her shopping cart with paper towels, dish soap, a gallon of bleach and a mop.

"You gotta git anything, Bucky?"

"Maybe some shavin' cream. I might could use some shavin' cream."

Lula headed down an aisle. "Pick me up a couple cans of dog food, will you, Bucky? Premium with chopped beef. You see it? It's got the golden retriever on the can."

Bucky put two cans of dog food in Lula's shopping cart. Lula picked up a toilet plunger and waved it like a wand. "You know, lookin' back, I wish I'd married that little hayshaker down in Dothan. Things might have been a lot different. But then, there's no way of knowin'. But I guess we'll know everything one day, Bucky, like the song says, when we meet on that beautiful shore."

I got a pleasant surprise one day, and then an unpleasant surprise, when Melissa Montague, the Mississippi Little Darlin', stopped by the Savage Ape joint with fruit and vegetables for the gorillas.

"The poor thangs ain't gettin' enough to eat! Okay, I feed 'em?" She handed the biggest gorilla some bananas and a head of lettuce. "Here's for you, Samson. And here's yours, Delilah. And Dizzy. Oh, you poor *thangs!*" She headed for the door. "Bye Samson! Bye Delilah! Bye Dizzy. Bye! Oh, I forgot to tell you. That little Margo's in a bad way. I went by the trailer last night. She…she don't have long to go. It's a shame."

Melissa was teary eyed and I figured, now's is my chance. She started to leave once again and I grabbed her and made a lunge for her mouth, but she easily wrenched herself away from me. The woman was animal strong.

"Jerzy, I'm gay!"

"What? What do you mean?"

"I'm gay. Electra and I…"

"Oh, my God! I'm sorry. I didn't know…"

"It's okay. I'm sorry too. Look, I gotta go. I'll see you…"

The next day I went by Lula's trailer and sure enough, it was perfectly true, what Melissa had said about Margo. She was curled up in a ball, whining softly to herself. Lula was sunk in gloom. "I took Margo to the vet yesterday," she said.

"And?"

"Canine heartworm."

"Canine heartworm? Well, maybe you can—"

"No, she's too far along. There's nothin' they can do."

Three days later Bucky, Electra, Melissa, Lula and I went out to bury little Margo. We were somewhere in

Arizona. We stood on a wooded knoll overlooking the desert, and Bucky dug a shallow grave. Melissa was crying so hard she had to go back to the car. Lula, sobbing, held the dead dog in her arms, then she placed the little body gently into the grave. I covered the body over with earth. Electra was crying softly. Bucky tried to comfort her with a pat on the arm, but she pulled away.

"Would y'all mind," Lula murmured. "I want to be alone with her for a few minutes."

I walked off a few paces and Bucky and Electra joined Melissa in the car. Pretty soon Lula motioned for me to come back. She handed me a homemade wooden cross and I tapped it into the ground with a rock. Lula coiled up Margo's leash and placed it on top of the grave.

"Goodbye, Pumpkin."

Bucky and I continued to follow Lash LaRue's itinerary in *Billboard*, and Bucky got excited every time Lula handed out mail, hoping he'd hear from Lash, but there was no letter. More than once we thought we'd catch up with Lash, and we almost did, in San Berdoo, but somehow he slipped away. It seemed that Lash was always one town ahead of us, always just out of reach, a star fading on the horizon, a mirage in the desert, a phantom, an apparition, a nemesis beyond the setting sun.

Right after we buried little Margo, Eric caught Electra and Melissa *flagrante delicto* and beat the hell out of the Electrifying Enchantress. Electra went to the hospital and came back with her left arm in a cast and her jaw wired shut.

Melissa went crazy. She buzzed her hair, cut it all off. She looked like a girl commando, like Joan of Arc. Still, she was pretty fetching. But you could see she was bent on revenge. And two days later Dickie the midget found Eric dead in his trailer. He'd been stabbed with one of his finely balanced throwing knives.

Lula got right on top of things. "We can't have the police here," she said. Bucky and I rolled Eric's body up in a rug and put it in the trunk of the Cadillac. It was time for burial detail once again. We were now somewhere in New Mexico. We drove out to a spot Lula knew about, Bucky and I, Lula, Electra and Dickie. Dickie was pretty broken up, but Eric the Knife was a rotten person and the rest of us were happy and relieved to be rid of him. Out of respect for Dickie's feelings I placed Eric's *How to Win Friends and Influence People* book on his chest before Bucky and I covered the grave over with dirt.

Then we heard that Electra and Melissa were leaving the carnival together, and that they were headed for Ottumwa. I don't think anybody was really surprised. I caught up with Electra at her trailer.

"Bucky asked me to apologize," I began, "for putting those moves on you, I mean. He didn't know you were…"

"Gay? Is that what you mean? Gay? You think I'm gay? I'm not. I'm not a lesbian. I'm not gay, Jerzy. I'm not."

"Then why—"

"Melissa? It's hard to explain. She ain't my boyfriend, but it feels like she's my boyfriend. She's kind and sweet and gentle. Love don't have to always be about sex, Jerzy. And it don't gotta be between a man and a woman, neither. It's just gotta be love. I don't know how to explain it. I guess what it comes down to is that Melissa is the only boyfriend I ever had who didn't beat the cowboy shit out of me."

I left the carnival two or three weeks later at Show Low, Arizona. I don't know what came over me. I guess my feet must have sprouted wings once again. I had the afternoon off so I walked into town and went to a bar. I ordered a beer, and as I looked at my reflection in the mirror, I realized—I'm not going back! It happened that suddenly.

When I got back to Clear Lake it was as if I'd never left. The plain still stretched out unendingly and the corn still whispered at night. I thought Chubby Thorvaldsson would be ready to send me to Bolivia in a box, but it turned out that Roddy had put in a word for me while I was gone: he's a good man but he needs to be on a longer tether and that sort of thing. The upshot of it was that Chubby put me in a halfway decent tractor and started me running down to El Paso, Laredo and Del Rio.

10

Chubby Thorvaldsson, my boss, was a good egg. You didn't have to call in every five minutes with your "twenty", and he understood that when you got down to Laredo or Brownsville you might want to spend a day or two across the border in Nuevo Laredo or Matamoros in the cantinas with the girls.

But he did want you to run miles, and to implement this program he handed out speed like candy. At the start of each trip, after you picked up your running money and went out to your rig, you were sure to find an envelope full of Los Angeles Turnarounds—white pills with a crude cross in the center—taped to the dash.

And so it began, *the Amphetamine Circus...*

Chubby had a perky little wife named Alice whose job it was to beguile Chubby's harried, sleep-starved drivers and serve as their "candy girl". I'd get back to Clear Lake after a week on the road, utterly frazzled and exhausted, and typically, moments after I got back to my digs and crashed, Chubby would send Sweet Little Alice Blue Gown over to perform her magic. Alice was a consummate actress. She'd barge right into my room where I was sleeping. "Oh, hi Jerzy! I didn't think you'd be asleep. I brought you a Coke from Tastee Freez." She'd sit on the edge of the bed in her shorts and break a Los Angeles Turnaround in half and drop it into my Coke. "A little something to brighten you up…"

Moments later I'd be sitting up in bed, alert as a squirrel. Sleep? *Ridiculous!* Who needs sleep? Why sleep when there's so much to *do?*

At this juncture Alice would take my hand and put it inside her halter and kiss me passionately, at the same time dropping the other half of the pill into my Coke. Then she'd pull away and pretend frustration. She wanted me desperately but there was no *time.* Chubby had a load of corn that had to be in Del Rio *yesterday!*

Then, after straightening her clothes and brushing back her hair, she'd hand me a fat envelope—my running money, plus another envelope filled with driver's little helpers, my pills for the trip.

Before many months went by I was hallucinating freely. On the road I saw all kinds of things that weren't there. A bridge in the middle of a cornfield, apparitions of overpasses emerging from fogbanks and disintegrating like sand castles, ghost cityscapes, phantom strip malls, domed palaces and massive Toltec heads by the side of the road. Familiar sections of highway magically transposed themselves from one city to another, accompanied by shimmering mirages of Dairy Queens and dissolving mountain peaks. Trees burst into flames and puffy cloud formations became enormous faces in the sky—some of them smiling, some of them weeping. And in my mirrors I saw shadows of wings, avenging angels leering from lascivious billboards, false dawns of Burger Kings and vanishing A&W Root Beer stands.

I couldn't eat. I must have lost twenty pounds. My heart was pounding like crazy. In order to come down enough to grab a few winks at a truck stop or a rest stop, I'd drink, usually from a pint of vodka or Jim Beam that I kept in the glove compartment, my "sleep medicine". After two or three hours of fitful dozing, all the while grinding my teeth, I'd pop a couple of Los Angeles Turnarounds, washing them down with vodka or whiskey, and get back on the road.

In May, Roddy had a blowout with Maryann and quit the Bookmobile job at the Mason City Public Library. He went back to work for Chubby and we began running together, mostly down to Laredo, Brownsville and Del Rio. Of course we went across the border to Nuevo Laredo and Matamoros, and especially to the Boystown at Ciudad Acuña, and our stays began to extend to two or three days or more in the cantinas with the girls.

A Little Madness in the Spring, you might say.

Now that Roddy was back on the road, he really cowboyed up—the red bandana, the ten-gallon hat and the embroidered shirts, just like the old days. And a brand new pair of hand-tooled Lucchese caiman belly boots that set him back a grand. Roddy, in his finery, looked like he'd just stepped off the set of *310 to Yuma*, and I was back to being the poor relation in my Long Haul t-shirt and my grimy Schneider National baseball cap.

The Boystown in Acuña was off by itself, an amazing whirligig of shooting lights that was almost a separate little pueblo at the end of a long dusty dirt road. You'd walk into a cantina like the Palacio de Oro, the Gold Palace, push through the swinging doors, and there they were, the whores, huddled in the booths, jabbering like schoolgirls, waiting patiently for their prince to come along. *"Pasale, guero. No tenga verguenza!"*

Boystown—especially the Boystown in Acuña—was to me the holy city, my Lhasa, my Maccu Picchu, my New Jerusalem, and a perfect place for Pinocchio and Lampwick to transform themselves into donkeys. The lurid neon signs, the sizzling taco pushcarts, the tiny *Indios* with their beads and Chiclets, the gaunt street dogs that patrolled like hyenas—it was a sordid world, raw and unadorned, but it was also a human world, human in a way that America is not and maybe never was. I adored the magnificent desolation of Boystown—the street-level communion, the bottom-of-the-bottle absolution, the ragged and desperate joy that can be known and shared only by those who have been factored out of the human equation. Boystown was an oasis in the American Desert, a place where a lonely man could find sex, comradeship— and even what the world calls love.

At the Durango Club, Blanca stuffed my mouth with kisses. She was a real blonde and claimed to be from Argentina, but it's more likely she was the half-American daughter of a whore. We spent hours in the booth, kissing, *besitos*, little kisses—peck, peck, peck—like two lovebirds. She would barely open her mouth. She'd allow me to feel her little *chiches* under her blouse, but I couldn't get her to go to the room.

In fact, I never saw her go to the room, on the nights, I mean, when she was sitting with other hombres, usually American truck drivers or soldiers. While the other girls at the Durango paraded to and from the *cuartos* in the rear with their jangling keys and their rolls of toilet paper, Blanca sat in her booth with her soldier boy of the moment or with me, chaste as a nun, dispensing affection in minute increments—*besitos*—little kisses—like penny candy.

Blanca's *compadre* Ofelia claimed that Blanca was a lesbian, but I didn't believe it. Ofelia was jealous, and besides Ofelia was a booze artist, a dedicated drunk who would have licked the spit off a dog's lips if she thought there was a drop of alcohol in it.

"Maybe she's a virgin," I suggested.

"*Claro*. And I am Pope Pius the Twelfth."

Ofelia had an American boyfriend, a Mayflower driver, a bedbug hauler, who showed up once in a while, and I'd sometimes help her write a letter to him in English. Then one night when the three of us were sitting in a booth, Blanca confided that she too had a sweetheart in the US, an old soldier from Tyler, Texas, supposedly a survivor of the Bataan Death March. She was living for the day when he'd would come to whisk her away to the US. She showed us his photo. He was old, all right. His tiny shrewd eyes were set in a seamy face that was creased and worn like an old catcher's mitt.

"He looks like a rhinoceros," Ofelia commented.

"Shut your mouth, you dirty pig!" Blanca snapped back

"What's his name?" I ventured.

"Papi."

Papi! That was a good one! I had to laugh, because the girls in the cantinas call every man "Papi". But Bianca was serious. She entirely believed in her dream, that someday Papi would come with all the pomp and grandeur of a great general entering a conquered city and carry her away to the land of milk and honey.

In any case, whenever I sat in the booth with Blanca I was careful to keep the drinks coming because she got fifty cents on each one and I figured she'd at least have the income from that while she waited for Papi to rescue her. Plus, I'd always leave a hefty tip at the end of our kissing session when I headed for one of the other cantinas and another girl—usually Marisa at the Adelita Club—whose dewy body would quench the fire so skillfully kindled by Blanca's little kisses, her *besitos*.

One day Roddy and I went looking for a *birria* restaurant in the "nice" part of town. We walked up and down the main drag. It was all curio shops, *farmacias* and splashy tourist bars. Suddenly Roddy ducked into a shop and came out with a cowboy hat. "Take this," he ordered. "I want you to have it. Go ahead, put it on!" He snatched off my grungy Schneider National hat and replaced it with the cowboy hat. "Get rid of that fucking thing!" he snapped. "Cowboy up, brother!" He handed my Schneider hat to a ragged *callejero* who accepted it without comment, then he led me to the window of a *loncheria* where we studied my reflection in the glass. Roddy seemed pleased with my new cowboy image.

"That's it. You gotta nurture your inner cowboy, man!"

A few shops away, the homeless man, wearing my discarded Schneider hat, was admiring his reflection in a store window. He was happy as a clam. It was a banner day for him. Roddy and I were both hung over so we went inside the *loncheria* and ordered *menudo*.

I sent Brenda a postcard from Acuña, and on the road, as the cities and towns fell away from the prow of the Freightliner, I thought about her, but New York seemed far away.

Marisa at the Adelita Club was my main squeeze in Ciudad Acuña. It was puppy love. She often took me to the room for free, *por amor*, as they say. Marisa had a friend, Evita, who, conveniently, was sweet on Roddy. We spent many nights with Marisa and Evita and sent them postcards from the road, from the magical, glamorous land of *Los Estados Unidos*, a world they would never see.

Coming back to Boystown was like coming home. We'd spend hours with our *novias*, sitting in the booths, mushing it up, playing the jukebox, and copying out the words to popular songs in Spanish, the language of the heart, and in English, as if we were children in grammar school. Evita was nearly a foot taller than Roddy. He was like a papoose in her hands. In order to keep the girls in a party mood, we'd put Los Angeles Turnarounds in their drinks. They'd stay up all night with us, swilling tequila and jabbering like monkeys.

We'd take our sweethearts to the movies and to dinner in the "nice" part of town. We had to pay the house a fee to ransom them out. It wasn't much, maybe ten dollars for the evening. Then we'd come back to the Adelita Club and spend the night. When it came time to say goodbye, Marisa would often burst into tears.

"*No te olvides de mi!*"

"You don't have to worry about that!"

I sent Marisa money from the road and wrote love letters to her in the truck stops. I had no dictionary, and because Spanish wasn't my language, I was very often not quite sure what I was saying, and this was a joy.

Roddy and I were running hard and drinking hard too in the cantinas. And then there was the speed. Our discussions were becoming more and more electric, more and more disjointed. Roddy was pilled up.

"What I'm seeing now is a multiplicity of events all going on simultaneously on several different levels that converge from point to point, from time to time, from epiphany to epiphany, themes within themes, the part for the whole, from the specific to the general, *rah-tah-tah-tah!* This is the theater of the mind, you understand."

Roddy and I went to visit Big Joe at the mink farm. We found him sitting in his battered green Chevy pickup reading a paperback novel. Big Joe Joplin's face was twisted into a permanent grimace. A North Korean bullet had passed through his cheek, taking with it a part of his jawbone, and leaving a deep crater on the left side. The skin below his left eye was stretched down over his shattered cheekbone, making the eye itself appear unnaturally large, like a great goggling fish eye peering out from under his Peterbilt baseball cap.

Big Joe offered me a drink from a pint of Jim Beam. I took it. Big Joe Joplin didn't look like a man you would want to refuse. He showed us around the place.

First we visited the pelting shed and then we walked between row upon row of wire cages, which housed, Big Joe said, some two thousand animals. The stink of them made my eyes water. The caged intensity, the furious cloistered metabolism of the mink farm was like the powerful electrical hum of a hidden generator. These frantic little animals with opaque black eyes were as speeded up as Roddy and myself. Their savage mink-hearts were pumping pure Crystal Meth. Paranoia was rampant, and it was well justified. Clearly, they seemed to know, each and every one of them, that their names were on the list of the proscribed. The mink farm was a prison, and everybody in it was on death row.

After the tour we talked trucks for a while, then Roddy and I left. We bought some beer and went over to Chubby's and sat in my rig and talked. *The Bridge*, Roddy's novel about his father, hinged on two bridges that had figured prominently in Big Joe Joplin's life. The bridges were pivotal points, metaphors of transition.

The first bridge was in Korea, at No Gun Ri, where American 7th Cavalry soldiers slaughtered more than two hundred Korean refugees, most of them women and children. Roddy's novel had its genesis one day when he overheard Big Joe tell the story to a customer in the pelting shed.

"My dad was nineteen years old, I heard him tell the guy. It was the summer of 1950, he said. The bridge at No Gun Ri was an arched concrete railroad trestle with two 100-foot- long underpasses. The people tried to hide in the tunnels. American soldiers were firing at them with M-1s and .30-caliber machine guns, and mortar rounds, too, were falling on them. It was a massacre. My father was a machine gunner. He got orders to fire and he fired. He said he just wanted it to be over. He held the trigger down and chopped them to pieces, women, children, mothers with babies…

"The shooting went on for an hour and a half, he said. Then he walked up on a pile of bodies at the entrance of one of the tunnels. A dead woman was holding her little girl in her arms. Part of the woman's head was missing. He picked up the little girl. A beautiful little girl, he said. She had a hole in her stomach and her left eye had been blown out. It was dangling on her cheek.

"In that moment, I heard my father say, everything went out of him, the incentive to win the war, the desire to kill the enemy soldiers, the patriotism, his whole sense of purpose. He just went dead. Somehow winning the war seemed meaningless beside the horror of this mutilated child, her body still warm in his arms, her blood dripping

145

on the sandy floor of the tunnel.

"What was the sense of it? I heard him say that he didn't fire his weapon after that, that he didn't much care anymore whether he lived or died. It was the only time I ever heard my father talk about the war."

Shortly after the massacre at No Gun Ri, Big Joe was wounded at the Naktong River and he came home, but he wasn't at all the same man who had gone off to war. He was plagued by nightmares and fits of crying, and he started drinking hard. He attended AA meetings, but it didn't help. He went through several jobs, with the drinking and all.

"He was running for the flatbed company out of Saint Paul. He was hauling heavy equipment. That was when he got involved with the woman from Baton Rouge. I was just a kid at the time. I didn't know much about it. That was when he took the running money. It was company money. They were going to run away together.

"He got down to this bridge over the Mississippi. He was on the way to get her, the woman from Baton Rouge. They were going to start a new life. He got out of his rig and walked out on the bridge. I don't know if he was going to jump or what. He was drinking, of course. I guess it was a moment of decision. He couldn't go through with it. Stealing the money, I mean, and running away with the woman from Baton Rouge.

"So he went back to the company and gave back the money. He'd already spent a lot of the money, hitting the bars and all. He was fired, of course, but they didn't press charges and they let him pay back the money over time. I don't know what happened with the woman from Baton Rouge, but he and Mom never talked much after that. Most of the time he just sat out there in the back yard in that old pickup truck, drinking whiskey and reading. Nobody around here would hire him to drive, so he started in with the mink farm. But even now, he spends most of his time out there in that old truck, reading."

"What does he read?"

"Louis L'Amour."

"Jesus!"

Roddy and Maryann got back together, then they had another fight and Roddy went on a bender in Minneapolis. I went back to running solo, and I pressured Chubby to give me the Del Rio runs exclusively so I could spend time with Marisa.

Then Roddy and I made what turned out to be our last trip together down to Del Rio. We spent a bunch of our running money in Boystown, and stayed off the road way longer than we should have. Roddy tried to smooth things over with Chubby on the phone, but Chubby was pissed off. He knew exactly what we were up to.

By way of a little comic relief, right after we arrived we got into a scrap with some livestock haulers at a dive called the Extranjero Club, and I lost my cowboy hat. After that I breathed a little easier because, unlike Roddy, I never was all that comfortable with the cowboy image.

But it was strange, the thing with Chubby. It was as if Roddy and I were repeating Big Joe's Baton Rouge folly, making off with the running money, hitting the bars and the rest of it—the escapade that ended with the decision on the bridge across the Mississippi.

Chubby threatened to fire us both but we knew perfectly well, as Chubby himself must have known, that he wouldn't go through with it. Drivers were hard to find, and anybody Chubby might dig up around Clear Lake was likely to be every bit as slipshod and irresponsible as Roddy and I were.

On that first night in Ciudad Acuña, Marisa and I had just gotten settled when I heard an agonized "Maiow!" It seemed to be coming from under the bed.

"*Qué cosa?*"

"It is the cat," Marisa explained. "She arrived here last week. She is *embarazado*—big with the *bebes. Me entiendes?*"

We heard more plaintive cries.

"Yes," I said. "I think she is having them right now. *En este momento!*"

And sure enough. We peeked under the bed and there they were—six tiny blind kittens mewling and peeping like baby birds, and the mother cat was busy gulping down the placenta.

Easter was right around the corner and Blanca had recently gotten a letter from the old soldier from Tyler, Texas, her Papi. She showed me Papi's letter and I translated it for her. Great news! It turned out that Papi was on his way to Boystown to fetch her. He was scheduled to arrive on Easter Day, in fact. Blanca was pissing her pants with excitement, and the girls at Durango Club began placing bets. Was Papi for real? Would he actually show up? Would he take Blanca away?

On Easter morning I went to Communion with Marisa, then we moseyed over to the Durango Club. I'd ransomed Marisa out of the Ad dita Club for the whole Easter weekend, so there was no problem about that. Roddy and Evita were there, at the Durango Club, and Ofelia, and Blanca, of course. We all sat in a booth with beers and waited while Blanca endured the taunts of the girls, who were undoubtedly jealous.

"He won't show!"

"He will!"

"He's a liar and so are you!"

"Go fuck your mother!"

Dreams do come true! Papi's arrival that Easter morning was like the coming of Christ, complete with palm leaves and glad hosannas, like the great god Bacchus returning to Rome from his conquest of India, drawn by tigers in a golden chariot. The old soldier pushed through the swinging doors of the Durango Club and stood there for a moment, blinking his tiny bright eyes. He was a *Gran Señor*, all right, truly majestic, a real *charro* in his embroidered jacket and fitted pants, black bow tie and wide-brimmed sombrero. His pencil line Clark Gable mustache was dyed black and his long white hair was tied in a ponytail. El Patrón! A mysterious figure, confident, savvy, complex, possibly dangerous, and certainly far more sophisticated than the bland Texas manner of his letter had suggested. I had no trouble believing the bit about the Bataan Death March. This man had been to hell and back.

Blanca leaped to her feet and gawked delightedly at the old man, then she flew into his arms, nearly knocking him down.

"Papi!"

After a tender embrace she led Papi to our booth and as the old soldier sat down with us, his arm around Blanca, I got a good look at this wrinkled, scaly relic. He was old, really old, gaunt, and the sharp, angular bones of his wrists were almost translucent. You felt on one hand that he might blow away on a breeze, but at the same time he seemed firmly rooted to the earth, like a serpent that sheds skin after skin and goes on living forever.

The bartender brought a bottle of Jose Cuervo and seven glasses. The old man poured, and you felt in that moment that he would never die, this *Gran Soñor* from Tyler, Texas, but would simply get older and older, wiser and wiser, more wrinkled, scalier and more majestic. After a few shots of tequila, Papi began to talk, in a monotone, like a priest reciting a litany, and suddenly we were on the island of Saipan in a madhouse of noise—mortars, tracers and machine gun chatter—ducking for cover behind smoldering hulks of Japanese tanks. The sun broiling down, our canteens empty… Piles of Japanese bodies everywhere and still they charged, leaping over their fallen comrades. And on the final day, when the Americans had won, the Japanese civilians…it was extraordinary. The women carried their children to the edge of a cliff that dropped a thousand feet to jagged rocks and jumped, holding the kids in their arms, and young girls too, scores of them, some barely in their teens, were diving off that cliff. It was the Bushido code—death before dishonor…

When Papi got up to go to the *excusados*, Blanca, who didn't understand English, asked me what we'd been talking about.

"Oh, nothing… the war."

"You see?" Ofelia snapped, smacking her glass down on the table. "Men! They love to play soldier! But it's the women who suffer. They kill us, they rape us… They'll cut the baby out of your womb! We lose our sons, we lose our brothers and our fathers. Goddamn men! They care only for their pricks and their guns and their wars! *Pfui!*"

Papi returned to the booth and he and Blanca went to the room. They didn't come back, and they didn't come back. We finished off the tequila.

"You don't suppose he had a heart attack…" Roddy ventured.

"No," Marisa said thoughtfully. "It probably takes him a while to get the damn thing up…"

Our last night in Boystown featured a bravura performance by Marisa's friend Ofelia that filled me with respect for her. Ofelia's *trocero*, the bedbug hauler, had thrown her over for a floozy who worked at the Gold Palace. Desolate and even drunker than usual, Ofelia hired the mariachis to play while she sang lead, emoting freely, pouring out her woe. Outside the open door of the cantina the menudo man trudged past with his wooden yolk and dangling kettles. You could hear roosters crowing. The cantina was deserted except for a few whores snoring in their booths and the bartender polishing his eternal glass. If she'd been born in America, Ofelia would have been married by now, driving a Volvo, juggling a baby or two, shopping at the supermarket, but fate had decreed that she serve out her time in a whorehouse in Ciudad Acuña. Standing up to the music, she belted out song after song, pissing away her night's earnings as dawn came up like a flaming circus and the silvery trumpets of the mariachis showered despair over it all.

I sent Marisa a postcard from Oke City: "I miss you.

Como está Evita? Roddy says hello to her. And to you. *Como van los gatitos?* How are the kittens?" And then—"*Yo te quiero…*" What the hell!

By June I had close to two thousand bucks stuffed under my mattress. My bed was getting lopsided, which didn't matter because I never slept in it anyway. Roddy had been driving off and on, in between spats with Maryann, but he was drunk most of the time now and helping out at the mink farm, so I was pretty much running solo.

On the road, the hallucinations were getting worse, and they had taken a sinister turn. I saw graveyards everywhere, white crosses, and severed arms and legs impaled on barbed wire. It was as if I'd been at Verdun and Chateau-Thierry in another life, and now a secret door had been forced, unleashing a flood of racial memories. I was okay as long as I kept moving, but the visions came thicker and faster when I stopped, during the brief intervals when I was off the road. Somehow the forward motion, on the road, kept them at bay, but when I stopped they rushed in with overpowering force.

In early August, as my sister's wedding approached, I was on the way home from Del Rio. At a rest stop on the I-35, north of Des Moines, as I was walking back to my rig, I stumbled into a forest of white crosses. An instant later the cemetery began burping up its dead. German soldiers. They were dead and I was alive, but they had the remedy for that, didn't they? Bullets began snapping in the air around my head. Then a huge German Cyclops with Big Joe's distorted face and a single goggling eye lunged at me with a bayonet. *"I'll have your bones to make my bread!"*

I felt myself running with lazy looping strides, like a diver wading in a kelp forest. People with au gratin faces that melted like cheese sandwiches were watching me closely. Gestapo? Mind agents? I had to get back to the rig. The rippling air was thick with entities, ghostlike, overlapping, intertwined, and a million voices, all gabbling at once. *What were they saying?* I couldn't sort it out, yet it seemed to me that my life depended on it. I had to find out what they were saying. *I had to break the code.*

Somehow I got back to Clear Lake. I parked the rig in the yard and called Roddy from a phone booth on Clear Lake's main drag and he came to get me in Big Joe's pickup. As frightened as I was, I had to laugh. Roddy, sitting behind the wheel, looked exactly like a big red lobster. He was holding the steering wheel with his claws. His eyes, protruding on stalks, seemed to be mocking me, as if he'd transformed himself into a lobster on purpose, as an elaborate practical joke.

Roddy parked the truck near a little marsh just outside of town. Huge waves of distortion rippled the sky and the air around me as we walked out into the ankle-deep water. There were trees, but I didn't dare look at them. I thought they might see me, and I was afraid of what they might say to me.

We sat down in the shallow water among reeds and cattails and Roddy handed me a bottle of tokay. He ordered me to drink it as fast as I could, and then cracked open another bottle. Gradually, as the warm sweet wine began to bring me down, I became aware of the idiotic quacking of ducks that were paddling merrily around nearby. There were red-winged blackbirds, too, flitting among the cattails.

A flock of Canada Geese passed overhead, very high, but we could hear them honking as they sped along, cutting through the air in perfect V-formation. I was aware of Roddy's voice droning on as if he were reciting poetry: "The geese fly south in the winter and north in the summer, sometimes all the way to Canada and Alaska. Birds on the east coast will head out over the Atlantic and swing down around Bermuda, riding a tailwind. Down there they'll pick up the trades and that takes them to South America..."

How *simple* life was. Simple, yet beautifully intricate and interconnected. I stole a glance at a tree. It was no longer threatening. Instead, it was transparent. I could see tiny luminous particles flowing up through the trunk into the branches and twigs and into the capillaries of the leaves. It was a symphony, orderly, measured, majestic.

Pretty soon Roddy, wet as he was, went off to buy more wine, leaving me in my puddle with the frogs and water birds. I wasn't afraid anymore. *The geese fly south in the winter and north in the summer.* Of course. Life is simple. Birth, copulation, death, preferably in that order. The heart circulates the blood and the stomach digests. It's all automatic and ordained. No fuss, no worries, just hop up on a lily pad and croak. Respiration, circulation, salivation. The stars wheeling around the earth's cosmic axis and wigglers swarming in a drop of water. There was nothing to understand, nothing to realize and nothing to get.

My tour of duty in Clear Lake was over. It was time to spread my wings and fly back to New York.

11

At the Mason City airport I boarded a Continental flight to La Guardia. I had my nest egg, two thousand bucks in Benjamins, in my wallet. I took a taxi to lower midtown Manhattan and checked into the historic Wolcott Hotel on 31st Street, just off 5th Avenue, where American literary lioness Edith Wharton had once lived. Perhaps she'd even written *The Age of Innocence* there, her famous chronicle of a glittering bygone age.

My room was comfortable to say the least—plush carpeting and leather-upholstered chairs, a huge desk and Wilem De Kooning wallpaper, all very Ecole Des Beaux-Arts and *fin de siecle*. I plunked my typewriter down on the massive walnut desk. It looked rather lonely there, and for some reason, at that moment, I thought of Big Joe Joplin, the old truck driver, sitting in his battered pickup drinking Jim Beam and thinking about the woman from Baton Rouge, or maybe about the faces of the dead children at No Gun Ri, while he waited for the whiskey river to carry him away.

On 5th Avenue I bought some clothes, nothing too fancy, a pair of pants and a Tommy Hilfiger shirt. I also bought a three-piece suit—and a new toothbrush. Crisply attired in my Calvin Klein jeans and a Tommy Hilfiger shirt, I took a taxi to the Village to look for Brenda. I opened the door of the Angels Camp Tavern. No Brenda.

"Brenda? I don't know any Brenda."

"Vodka martini, three olives."

"Oh, *Brenda!* Why didn't you say so? Sure, I know Brenda. No, I ain't seen her."

Hal, I learned, had joined the Merchant Marine, several months ago.

I went by Brenda's digs, the rat hole on Charles Street. The woman who opened the door smelled like sour sweat and stale beer. Brenda? Haven't seen her. Nope! Who wants to know? Oh, *that* Brenda! You mean Brenda! *Brenda* Brenda! No, she moved out. Her and that cat. Oh, weeks ago. Maybe months. *Say, you want a drink?*

At Washington Square Park it was just the usual refugees from the storm. A madwoman counting her pigeons, the eternal chess players, and a couple of scarecrows passing a jug tightly wrapped in a brown paper bag. No Brenda. And then, as a street preacher finished his spiel and skulked away, I saw her, sitting on the edge of the fountain pool with the yellow cat in her lap.

She was glad to see me and yes, she'd gotten my postcards, and yes, she'd moved out, and no she wasn't homeless, the cat was just keeping her company.

"Would you like a drink?"

We finished off the bottle of Southern Comfort she had in her purse then took a taxi to her new place on Spring Street and I met her roommate, Trish. There were empty bottles everywhere. Brenda's sketchbook lay open on the floor. Charcoal drawings of her cat, Taffy. Not bad. Cityscapes, empty streets, like Utrillo.

I always envied Utrillo. First he had his mother, Suzanne Valadon, to take care of him, and later his wife managed his affairs and, drunk and half crazy as he was, he was free to spend his days painting. Maurice Utrillo: he knew the lonely streets.

I was holding the jack, so I took the girls' shopping list

to a neighborhood grocery and bought beer, wine and Southern Comfort, enough alcohol for a block party.

Taffy, Brenda's yellow cat, had smoky green eyes, flecked like a lion's eyes, unfathomable, cold. *Taffy*. Just like a girl to name a cat Taffy! What a stupid name for a carnivorous creature that was essentially a miniature lion. If our sizes had been reversed, Taffy would have eaten me with no more malice than a human might display toward a ham and cheese sandwich. Oh, she was nice enough—purring and rubbing against you—when she wanted something, if she thought there was something in it for her. I thought of Marisa's under-the-bed cat and the scrawny kittens at the Adelita Club. Compared to them, Taffy was a fat cat indeed. Even the hardscrabble life she shared with Brenda was a picnic compared to Mexico, where an unwary cat might well end up as a *chimichanga*.

Just before closing time we went back to the bar and we belted them down, with me paying. Finally, after making a dinner date with Brenda, I left a couple of twenties on the bar and I wobbled back to my hotel. I was no stranger to booze, but there was just no way I could have kept up with those two.

The next morning, after breakfast at the hotel, I dropped by the New York Public Library. Edith Wharton's book, *The Age of Innocence*, wasn't my cup of tea, certainly, but because I was curious, I found a copy on the shelves and leafed through it. *"Then stay with me a little longer," Madame Olenska said in a low tone, just touching his knee with her plumed fan. It was the lightest touch, but it thrilled him like a caress."*

I strolled around midtown Manhattan, looking for ambiance. A light rain was beginning to fall. So this was the Writer's Life! I felt disconnected. Was this what Joyce experienced on his strolls through Dublin? Or Dickens in London? The world was an egg and I was walking around it, tapping the shell with my cane. There must be a crack somewhere, a chink in the armor, a weak spot where I could force my way inside. *Here?* Here? *Maybe here!* No one likes to be outside, in the rain. I couldn't get a footing. Everything was slipping away from me, or I from it. I seemed to be water skiing over the graves of dead children. Was this the Writer's Life I'd dreamed of? Oh dear sweet Jesus, *Madame Olenska, do please touch my knee with your pluméd fan!*

Back at the hotel once again, there was a telephone message from Brenda canceling our dinner date for the following night. I tried to reach her without success. Then, three nights later, she called, half in the bag, slurring her words: "Yes, Jerzy, I *do* want to go to dinner with you. I'm sick of being an alcoholic. I want to do things and go places. I've been thinking about going back home, too. I could go to meetings again. Maybe I can clean up. 'Don't drink, find a sponsor, go to meetings, ask for help.' That's what they tell you. That's how it works. But, Jesus, how do you get past that first step? *Don't drink…* "

The dinner, our date. Where did we go? Triomphe, on West 44th Street, of course! I wore my new three-piece suit and Brenda wore a simple blue dress and a white angora cardigan with tiny pearl buttons. I ordered the Perrier Jouet Grand Brut Champagne, and for the meal, a hearty Chateau de Clairefont Bordeaux 1968, since we planned to order the filet mignon au poivre with mushroom demi-glace, creamed English peas and grilled radicchio.

But things went badly right from the get-go.

"Why couldn't we just go out for a pizza? I don't feel comfortable here."

"Jesus Christ, Brenda, I wanted you to have fun. I wanted you to have some happiness in your life."

She took her bottle of Southern Comfort out of her purse and swallowed a big gulp.

"You don't have to do that, for crying out loud."

I ordered another bottle of Perrier Jouet Grand Brut. But the bubbly, as I should have known, only made things worse.

Brenda picked at her food. She was looped.

"Why did we have to sit in a booth? Are you ashamed to be seen with a cripple?"

"Look Brenda," I said, as I deftly speared a Portobello mushroom, "can't we just be friends? What's so difficult about that? I have feelings for you. I'm not saying I'm in love with you, but I'm not saying I'm not either. Why don't you try the cannelloni au gratin?"

"*I don't want your pity!*"

"You know, the asparagus salad with truffles vinaigrette looks pretty good. I was thinking, too, that next time we might want to order the rock shrimp and basil ravioli. Or the seared coriander crusted Australian lamb rack with *foie* stuffed prunes, saffron couscous, mango chutney and—"

"*Shit! Shit! Shit!* I need a drink. A *real* drink!"

What was it, exactly? What was it that I saw in her? It was Brenda's vulnerability, her woundedness, that drew me to her. I had the crazy notion that I could pull her up somehow, that I could "rescue" her. It was cockeyed, I knew that, but I couldn't get over it. I'd repair her broken wings, heal her wounds, make her whole again. And then, cautiously, I'd open my hand and she'd fly away from me, full of hope, full of song.

Now she was crying in her onion soup.

"Jerzy, I'm sorry. I know you're not like Hal, and I appreciate that. But I've been hurt. I'm like a fawn. I'm ready to bolt, right this minute. I can't help it. I guess you and I will be like, as they say, two ships that pass in the night. And in my experience, there's goddamn few ships and a whole lot of night."

"Then why not take a chance?"

"*Forget it!* You're kind and gentle. You've got a nice smile and a good heart. I appreciate your offer of friendship, but I'm just not ready. I don't want anybody. Can't you understand that? *I don't want anybody!* I'm not ready for a relationship."

A fool and his money! The next morning in my hotel

room I checked my poke. It hadn't taken me long to go through the two thousand bucks. I had three Benjamins and some chickenfeed left, and I was determined to spend it foolishly. A grand gesture, a futile gesture.

An exercise in futility, I told myself, is the highest form of art.

I went to a florist shop on 5th Avenue and ordered five dozen roses. It came to $300. Back to the room. It was time to check out. My money was gone. I hadn't written a line. *The Writer's Life!* I hadn't even plugged in the typewriter.

I found Hal at the bar. He'd just gotten back in town that very day. Yes, he had work for me, and sure, I could crash on his floor. The Merchant Marine thing hadn't worked out. He'd jumped ship in Trieste and hitchhiked across Italy—well, that was another story.

"That's great, Hal!"

There might be some hope for Hal yet. He was finally finding something to write about. To celebrate, I bought us a round of drinks with Hal's money, a ten-spot I picked up off the bar.

"Cheers," he said uncertainly. "Well, when do you want to start?"

"How about now?"

"What's with the suit? Don't you want to change your clothes?"

"Fuck it!"

We went to a painting job on Sullivan. We were both drunk. I got paint all over my new suit. We went back to the bar. I looked a fright. My suit was splattered with paint. My long curls were popping out of a paper painter's hat I had crammed assways on my head.

Just then Brenda walked in. For the first time since we'd met, she seemed sober.

"Thanks for the roses."

"You're welcome."

"You're crazy, do you know that? I came to say goodbye. I'm leaving town today. I called the hotel but they said you'd checked out."

She showed me a bus ticket.

"Broken Bow, Nebraska. That's my hometown. Don't tell me you've been to Broken Bow."

"I'm a goddamn truck driver. I've been to every town in the United States."

"Why did you send me those flowers?"

"I'm glad you asked me that. I'm going to tell you. I think the world has undervalued you, and you've undervalued yourself. I think you're beautiful, inside and out."

Hal and I ordered drinks at the bar. My beautiful bird had flown. It was the front money we were spending. I didn't care. My suit was ruined. It didn't matter. Nothing mattered.

It was August twenty-fifth, almost time for my sister's wedding.

12

The three of them—my mother, my father, and my sister Erin—met me at the door of the house on Pioneer Street, looming before me like the Three Fates of Greek legend, their faces grim as death.

The moment I saw them standing there I realized that I'd made a mistake in returning to Cooperstown for the wedding, but of course it was too late to turn back. They were staring at me in disbelief, as if I were something that had crawled out from under the wallpaper. I was wearing my old Army khaki shirt with the shadow of my missing corporal stripes on the sleeve and my Mercury Movers winged-foot hat. My hair fell in ringlets to my shoulders.

A bit later, as I was stepping out of the shower, I heard my mother going on in the kitchen. "My God, Rufus, he looks a fright! What did we do wrong? Did you see his hair? Lie down with dogs and rise up with fleas, they say! I give up. I just plain give up. What's the use? What's the use of any of it? It's a losing battle, I'll tell you that! Well, what can you do? What can any of us do? Take it one day at a time, I guess. The world's a closed shop, Rufus! Sure as you live and breathe! It's a stacked deck! You can't win! You just can't win!"

My father made no response. I couldn't see him, but I

figured he was in the living room hiding behind his newspaper as usual, Gargantua in chains. I could hear him sucking at his loose front teeth, which was normally his only response to my mother's Litany of Despair. A few moments later, as I was getting dressed, I heard him whistling *Begin the Beguine,* and I knew he was taking out the garbage. My father always whistled *Begin the Beguine* when he took out the garbage.

After supper my father called me aside, in the back yard out by the tulip bed. I thought at first he was going to hit me, or maybe run me down about my shaggy appearance. But no, he shot me a tricky wink, and for an eerie instant I thought he was going to tell me a dirty joke. But instead, he leaned close, plucked at my sleeve, and with another wink and a delighted smile, he confided: "Tomorrow's Thursday."

I didn't know what to say, except, "Yeah, Dad, tomorrow's Thursday."

"*Thursday,*" he repeated.

"Thursday…" I wasn't following him at all.

"Don't you remember, Son? Thursday," he burbled, his eyes radiant half-moons of beatific joy, "Thursday is…*Bean Day!*"

Thursday is Bean Day! Of course! How could I have forgotten? Thursday is Bean Day! It had always been so, since the dawn of creation, since Adam was formed of dust and spit, since Jurassic time, since the first slimy sea-thing spouted legs and walked upon dry land. *It would always be so.* The pyramids might crumble, the earth might spring out of its orbit, our galaxy itself might plummet into a black hole, but Thursday would always be Bean Day at the Mulvaneys.

Bean Day! Every Thursday, week after week, month after month, year after year, at the house in Cooperstown, we ate baked beans, Heinz Baked Beans with Tomato Sauce. And Friday… Friday it was Mrs. Paul's Fish Sticks, and Monday, fried Spam. Tuesday, Vienna sausages, and Wednesday, Hormel Corned Beef Hash, which we called "red flannel hash." My mother, in fact, kept a schedule of the meals and the days taped to the refrigerator. *Lest we forget!*

I often wondered, since my father was so crazy about what he called "your mother's baked beans," why we couldn't have had baked beans twice a week, say on Saturday instead of the tuna casserole, but I also knew perfectly well that it was fruitless to suggest such a thing. *Baked beans? On Saturday? Ridiculous!* One didn't, you see. You didn't do that. It simply wasn't done.

After I'd gone back into the house and helped my mother with the dishes, she showed me a glass jar next to the stove filled with individually wrapped Hall's Mentholyptus Cough Drops. She told me this: "Every Wednesday night after *Wheel of Fortune* we each have one of these and then we play three hands of gin rummy."

We got settled in the living room, my father in his easy chair and my mother perched next to him on the couch. I sat in a rocking chair facing them. On the wall above their heads was the famous Grant Wood print, *American Gothic*, the solemn father with his three-tined pitchfork and the stoic maiden daughter with her cold, vacuous, expression. I was expecting the worst, but my mother's mood had inexplicably brightened somewhat.

"Guess what, Jerzy," she said, beaming at me proudly. "I can recite the names of all the Presidents, the Books of the Bible, the names of the Seven Dwarfs, the letters of the Greek alphabet, and lots more. And all the counties in New York, too!" And she began to reel them off: "Otsego, Oswego, Chenango, Chautauqua, Cattaraugus, Cayuga..."

My father, responding as if on cue, began drumming his fingers nervously on the coffee table, and muttered, with a weary shake of his head, *"Jesus! Oh, Jesus, Jesus, Jesus!"*

It's classic in families that seemingly trivial issues can trigger long buried pockets of resentment and anger. This was the case with the issue of my hair. If I appeared at the wedding with that fright wig, my sister protested, everything would be ruined. The family insisted that I get a haircut, but I put my foot down and wouldn't budge. Ridiculous as my position was, I defended it with fanatic zeal.

On Friday we all went for drinks and dinner to the historic Otesaga Hotel on Otsego Lake where Fosley Brandt, my sister's husband-to-be, was staying. I didn't have any decent clothes to my name, but I was able to fit into a pair of my father's trousers and a pair of wingtip shoes. The sport coat, however, was too small, so we went to Willoughby's Men's Shop on Cooperstown's Main Street where my father grudgingly shelled out for a proper sport coat for me.

It seemed strange to be going out as a family, not just to the Otesaga, but out to dinner at all. During our growing up years my father took us occasionally to the Cooperstown Diner on Main Street, across from Smalley's Theater and Doubleday Field, but that was about it. At the Cooperstown Diner we invariably ordered the Meatloaf Special, and sometimes we had apple pie a la mode for dessert.

Fosley Brandt came from a "good" family, a *manufacturing family*, my mother reminded us as we drove to the hotel. The way my mother uttered the phrase "manufacturing family", it was as if the phrase "manufacturing family" conferred an elegant world of privilege and decorum from which we were of course excluded.

This impression was further reinforced, as my father was parking the car, when my mother, still going on about Fosley Brandt's family, swiveled in her seat to peer at Erin and myself, and rolling her eyes and wringing her hands, whispered bitterly, "I don't suppose they'd have anything to do with *us!*"

I'd never been to the Otesaga, except at the service entrance, delivering groceries with my neighbor Vic Van Zandt when I was fourteen and we both worked at

Guido's Market on Main Street. No one I knew had ever gone there, including my parents. The Otesaga was for the tourists, for the summer people, or for "quality folks".

Fosley Brandt seemed like a thoroughly decent guy. There was nothing patronizing or condescending about his manner. I had fastened my offending hair in a neat ponytail, and Fosley, as far as I could tell, found nothing untoward about my appearance.

Fosley Brandt and I quickly fell into a conversation about the multiplicity of ethnic neighborhoods in New York City, and when my mother butted in with, "My God, you couldn't pay me to live there," Fosley deftly parried her thrust with a smile and a nod, and shot me a quick reassuring glance.

My parents, after considerable debate, both ordered Old Fashions. My sister ordered a gin and tonic, and Fosley a whiskey sour. In order to seem somewhat chummy with a man who I now perceived as a possible ally, I ordered a whiskey sour also.

Just the same, I was so damned uncomfortable that for a giddy instant I considered simply bolting out the door. My father had given me a twenty-dollar bill earlier. I could have made my way back to New York without too much trouble. By this time in my life I was a real virtuoso when it came to sprouting winged feet, a regular Mr. Bojangles. But then I would have missed Aunt Mizpah, who was on her way to Cooperstown from Brandon.

The drinks arrived and my father proposed a toast. *"To the bride and groom! Happiness and long life!"* My mother laughed sardonically, as if commenting on the utter impossibility of such an outcome. My father gave me a hopeless smile and sucked at his loose teeth, a habit which always drove my sister wild.

"Rufus! *Stop it!*" Erin snapped, kicking him under the table. Even as a child Erin had called our father by his first name.

My sister Erin, unlike me, did everything right. She

went to nursing school and then worked at the Mary Imogene Basset Hospital in Cooperstown. Then she met Fosley Brandt, a mathematics professor at Russell Sage College in Albany, the very same college my mother had attended before meeting Rufus Mulvaney, the railroad brakeman's son from Oneonta. With the marriage to Fosley Brandt, it was as if Erin were completing my mother's destiny, which had somehow gone awry when she married Rufus Mulvaney.

After we'd finished our drinks and my father ordered another round, I began to take heart. *It never hurts to blur the edges a little bit!*

Pretty soon my mother piped up: "What on earth has happened to books today? I get everything on the Bestseller List and there's none of it worth a hill of beans. So many characters, and you don't for the life of you know what's what. And half of it's *dirt!* Well, what can you do? You can't win. You…just…can't win."

My mother was an avid reader. All the books she read came from the Bestseller List. Every day she clipped the Bestseller List, along with the daily crossword puzzle, out of the newspaper.

I had definitely caught a little bit of a buzz, so I boldly countered: "Well, there are lots of other books. I mean besides the Bestseller List. You could always go back a little bit."

"Like what? Back where? What do you mean?"

"Back in time, I mean. Dickens, Dostoevsky, Joseph Conrad. Or Thomas Hardy, or Tolstoy, for example, or the Bronte Sisters…"

My mother was astonished. Her expression was pained, perplexed, incredulous, as if I'd been speaking Swahili. The problem, as I'd anticipated, was that these authors weren't on the Bestseller List, so they couldn't be considered. *Sorry, Fyodor!*

But now that I had her going I began to lay it on thick: "William Blake, Rabelais, Francois Villon… How about

Céline, *Mort à Crédit?* Or Genet, *The Thief's Journal?* Reaching back a bit further, there's the thirteenth century poetess Hadewijch of Antwerp, as well as Mechthild of Magdeburg and Angelus Sliesius."

My father looked at me sharply. I knew I should shut my trap but I was running with my tail up in the air. I could sense victory now and I plunged recklessly onward.

"Turning now to the courtly tradition, we have the Troubadors, Bertran de Born and Jaufré Rudel, and, of course, Chrétien de Troyes. A very fertile period. This was the time of the Minnesingers in Germany, you know, notably Wolfram von Eschenbach…"

My mother was almost in tears. She sat there dumbfounded, flabbergasted, her face crumpled like a muffin. For me, the exultation of triumph was brief. I was thoroughly ashamed of myself now. I felt chagrined to say the least. Filled with remorse, I tried to smooth things over with some giddy talk about the weather, but my mother, quite unexpectedly, bounced back.

"I'll bet you can't name the eleven Confederate States," she declared with a challenging gleam in her eye and a pugnacious set to her jaw.

I saw my chance to redeem myself and answered meekly that I most certainly could not.

"*I* can," she allowed. "South Carolina, North Carolina, Texas, Georgia, Virginia, Arkansas, Mississippi, Tennessee, Alabama, Florida and Louisiana!"

Now that my mother had started in with her memorized lists there was no stopping her. She reeled off the Six Nations of the Iroquois, the Twelve Tribes of Israel, then the names of all eight children of Rutherford B. Hayes, nineteenth President of the United States. Then, thoroughly enlivened by the alcohol, she boldly proclaimed that she could name thirty-two varieties of beans. And damned if she didn't pull it off:

"*Great Northern, Lima, mung, kidney, fava, cannelloni…*"

Although my mother's manner, whenever she recited

her lists, was completely ingenuous, I sometimes had the eerie feeling that she was subtly mocking us, and the world at large, by demonstrating that she could dedicate herself wholeheartedly to the achievement of a goal that was patently worthless, and this by way of shoring up and confirming her lifelong motto vis-à-vis the world: *"You just can't win."* It was as if she delighted in the uselessness and futility of it all.

I wondered too, as I started to say earlier, if my mother might not be envious of my sister, the child who had somehow usurped her destiny. This was the life that had been orchestrated for *her*, Ellen Smeisser Shimmersalz. Graduation from Russell Sage College, her trip to Europe, then marriage to a doctor or a lawyer, or at the very least to a proper university professor. Certainly there had been no place in this elegant scenario for rooting around among the turnips with the likes of the Mulvaneys.

And yet, here she was, Ellen Smeisser Shimmersalz, the Déclassé Diva from Brandon, marinating like an artichoke in the irony of it, in the almost cosmic irony of it all. Here, before her eyes, passed what might have been, what could have been, what should have been. Fosley Brandt was *her* intended, wasn't he? Not Erin's! But who then was this rough-cut lout of a Rufus Mulvaney, the telephone lineman who dropped out of school in the eighth grade? And this hooligan son with his horrid ponytail! What had she done to deserve this fate? What crime had she committed? What unspeakable transgression? How cruel the world was, how monstrous!

She didn't say any of this, mind you, but I could hear the gears meshing and whirring inside her head, and at that moment a sudden realization struck me. She was doing—mentally, at least—the same thing I'd been doing in New York! *She was writing a screenplay!*

She'd already shot the film, in fact, so to speak, and now she was cutting it together, a little snip here and a sprinkle of the old magic dust there.

This scene at the Otesaga, drinks in the grand dining room, with Fosley Brandt as the Archduke Franz Ferdinand and us, the Mulvaneys, as the ragged street urchins of Sarajevo with our snotty noses pressed against the window of the candy store, this scene was being processed and filed away—subtly altered and tricked up—for inclusion in my mother's *oeuvre complète*, her magnum opus, her scherzo scherzando—her Litany of Despair!

My sister and I got up and trekked to the restrooms in the lobby.

"Do you remember Butchie Bear?" I asked suddenly.

"*Butchie Bear!* What does that have to do with anything? How many times did you take LSD? No, don't tell me. I don't want to know."

"I'll wait for you out here," I said, sinking into a comfy padded bench.

"Good. Don't wander off."

Butchie Bear was one of my favorite childhood companions, a battered stuffed toy bear fitted with shiny red wheels. I rode Butchie Bear all around the house, especially in the kitchen where the smooth linoleum made for easy cruising. Butchie Bear was the warhorse on which I rode headlong into the maelstrom of flack generated by my mother's Litany of Despair.

Back at our table we all sat looking out at Otsego Lake. A soft summer breeze was fluttering the leaves of the trees, and the Chief Uncas, the Clark's sleek pleasure yacht, had just passed by, the waters of the lake playing through its quiet motors. Aboard would have been Honey Haverhill, Durwood Smythe-Davies, and Ambrose Clark, who owned the Chief Uncas. And Todd Darlington and his wife, Cornelia, née Vladimirovna, a Russian countess.

"Isn't this *grand?*" my mother remarked, with just the slightest hint of sarcasm in her voice. Slight, but it was there. It was as if she'd added: "Too bad we don't belong here!" It was as if we were a family of blind moles that had tunneled our way to the earth's surface for a brief respite in the sunlight before returning to the foul-smelling darkness of our abysmal subterranean lair.

My sister kicked me under the table and silently formed the words, "*Elias Howe*," with her lips. She was warning me that our mother was about to launch into one of her favorite harangues, the sad story of our hapless ancestor, Elias Howe, who invented the sewing machine, and the subsequent Howe-Singer controversy. And sure enough, off she went in her most anguished manner, spewing bitterness left and right, yet savoring every word. If Howe hadn't been shmeckled by Singer, my mother contended, "That could have been *us* sitting on the deck of the Chief Uncas in our tennis whites instead of Todd Darlington and that Russian woman!"

What she meant, of course, is that it *should* have been us. The implication was that something had gone terribly wrong in the past, and as a result we, the Mulvaneys, instead of claiming our glorious birthright, had been reduced to our present deplorable condition. *How the mighty have fallen!* We'd come *this* close to greatness; we'd missed getting on the train by the teensiest of hairsbreadths. We'd been derailed somehow by a random quirk of fate and had failed to keep our appointed rendezvous with destiny.

And now, of course, it was too late—far, far too late.

The facts of the case are fairly simple. Elias Howe, born in 1819 in Spencer Massachusetts, worked as a machinist in Boston and invented the sewing machine in 1845, but failed to protect his patent from imitators. Howe was portrayed by my mother and by the history books as a mechanical genius, but an impractical dreamer.

Now, along comes Singer—bold, charismatic, a Shakespearean actor and a flimflam man, a bigamist who fathered twenty-four children, a man who was used to living large and who didn't mind riding roughshod over everyone in his path. Briefly, Singer snagged the patent, raked in the dough, bought a mansion on Fifth Avenue, and became one of the Gilded Age's most flamboyant captains of industry. And today it's Singer's name that's associated with the sewing machine, not Howe's.

But that wasn't by any means the end of the fateful chain of circumstances, the way my mother told it. Singer took on as a partner one Edward Clark, a New York attorney, and together they made millions, Singer with his revolutionary new machine and Clark with a line of sewing thread. Edward Clark was the patriarch of the Clark family that in later years—that is, in our era—more or less owned Cooperstown, and the Chief Uncas, on whose deck fortune's favorites were at this very moment cavorting, was owned by Ambrose Clark, great grandson of Edward.

"Clark and Singer were very closely connected," my mother was fond of saying, "the sewing machine and thread."

The sewing machine and thread…

And then there was us—*the threadbare Mulvaneys!* The inescapable conclusion was that if that idiot Howe, that wide-eyed dreamer of an Elias Howe hadn't bobbled the ball, why we, the Mulvaneys, would have been in a fair way to live the life of luxury and ease which we so obviously and so richly deserved.

This was the case that my mother propounded with relentless enthusiasm, day after day, month after month, and year after year. It was the *irony* of it, the agonizing irony of what of might have been, of what could have been, of what *should* have been—this was the leitmotif to which my mother returned over and over. If only we'd been serfs and peasants plain and simple, right from the beginning and for all time, why, it wouldn't have been so bad. But it was this brush with greatness, this narrowly missed opportunity, that turned whatever sweetness we might have otherwise savored into the sourest of sour grapes.

"Well," she'd conclude, wringing her hands in that special hopeless way of hers, "what can you do? What can any of us do? Take the bitter with the better, that's all.

Take the bitter with the better!'

Nor was this the end of it. The idea that our family was irrevocably hexed-up, clearly established by the disastrous Howe-Singer affair—that was merely the underlying litigation, so to speak, of my mother's campaign to prove once and for all that nothing good could ever happen to any of us.

She would put herself on the witness stand and recall the fateful night she met Rufus Mulvaney at that dance at the Brandon Inn. She'd just returned from Europe where she'd gone for a sabbatical with her roommate Kay Dalrymple née Forsythe after the two of them had graduated from Russell Sage College in Albany. Subsequently, she'd learned from her sister, Aunt Mizpah, as the day of the dance drew near, that the trombone player had broken his elbow in a lacrosse match, and that consequently, the dance would have to be cancelled.

Then at the last moment somebody came up with a trombone player from Oneonta who happened to be in Brandon for his uncle's funeral. That substitute trombone player was, needless to say, none other than Rufus Mulvaney, the railroad brakeman's son, who was, in Aunt Mizpah's words, "a swell musician but an awful rake."

That night at the Brandon Inn, my mother related, she, my mother, got a little tipsy and began flirting with the guys in the band, something that, as Aunt Mizpah and Kay Forsythe sternly reminded her, "simply wasn't done."

But my mother, ultimately, blamed everything on *Begin the Beguine*. She ended up, Ellen, my mother, dancing several dances with Rufus between sets, dancing to *Begin the Beguine*. And that was what did it! She fell in love with the big oaf, as they danced to *Begin the Beguine,* and soon after that they were married, and my father gave up his musical career and took a job with the telephone company, and then I was born and then my sister, Erin.

My mother had certainly done her homework, I'll say that for her!

Not only that, but to make the irony even more delicious, it was at this very dance at the Brandon Inn that Kay Forsythe snagged her millionaire—hedge-fence homely, filthy rich Hebie Dalryrmple with his sleek Packard touring car.

Now she'd start in, my mother, with the "what-ifs." What if Whippoorwill Farm hadn't burned down and Grandma Maddalyn hadn't committed suicide by drinking Paris Green? Why, she, Ellen Shimmersalz, my mother, wouldn't have been orphaned and sent to live with Judge John S. Niedenthal, that's what.

And if she hadn't lived with the Judge and Aunt Izz during her growing-up years she wouldn't have gone to Russell Sage College and she wouldn't have met Kay Dalrymple née Forsythe and they wouldn't have gone to Europe together after graduation. And if she hadn't returned from Europe when she did with Kay, and if they hadn't gone to that dance at the Brandon Inn, and if the original trombone player hadn't broken his arm playing lacrosse, and if Rufus's Brandon uncle hadn't died, and if Rufus hadn't taken the place of the lacrosse-playing trombone player, then she would never have met Rufus, that telephone pole-climbing monkey, Rufus Mulvaney, the railroad brakeman's son from Oneonta, and she certainly would never have married him.

And so, you see, things might have been different. Could have been different. Would have been different. *Should* have been different.

And with this she would wring her hands once again in her whining, hopeless way and plunge even deeper into regret, remorse and despair—thoroughly enjoying every minute of it, of course—and like a drowning woman she'd try to drag the rest of us down with her.

It even got to the point where Erin, in later years, bought into this absurd scenario, hook, line and sinker, and began spieling it off to me in our cross-country phone conversations whenever I called to hit her up for a few bucks. "If Singer hadn't ripped Howe off for the patent, Grandma Mulvaney—Effie Robina Howe—wouldn't have had to work in that textile factory and she wouldn't have met Grandpa Sean Mulvaney, the railroad brakeman from Oneonta, and Rufus wouldn't have been born. But even if Rufus had been born—as he was—still, if the farm hadn't burned down and Ellen hadn't gone to live with Aunt Izz, and if she hadn't gone from there to college and to Europe and returned just when she did, and if the trombone player hadn't broken his elbow, and if Rufus hadn't replaced him, then Ellen might not have gone to that dance at the Brandon Inn because they would have called it off, you see, and if she hadn't gone to the dance, then she wouldn't have met Rufus, and they wouldn't have danced to *Begin the Beguine*, and she wouldn't have fallen in love with him, and if she hadn't fallen in love with Rufus, and married Rufus, then, well, maybe you and I...well, maybe I might have been Meg Ryan and you might have been Donald Trump!"

Anyway, it turned into a frightful ruckus, the business about my hair, with the wedding coming up and all. After we got home from the Otesaga, we went into the back yard to have it out, my sister and I. Standing next to our father's tulip bed, near the graves of our pets, Tippy and Mittens, we flew at each other.

"Jesus Christ, Jerzy! Have I ever asked you for anything? This is the most important day of my life. And you come here looking like a Gypsy! *Get a goddamn haircut!* Is that so much to ask? You know, you're just like *her!* Rain on everybody's parade! The dog in the manger, that's you. I hope you're proud of yourself! If you screw up my wedding, I'll never forgive you! You're the big New York intellectual now and we're dirt under your feet. Is that it? We're the provincials! Your poor relations from Cooperstown! *Shanty Irish!* We're the 'little people of the world!' That's the way you see things, isn't it? You're so full of shit! Growing your hair is your way of making a statement. Some kind of pseudo-existentialist bullshit! Jean

Paul Sartre and Albert Camus. Jesus Christ! Why don't you go to France with the rest of the pansies? Go back to New York. *Get the hell out of here!* Really. I mean it. Go back to New York!"

Not one thing had changed at Willy Witherspoon's Barbershop on Walnut Street. It was a tableau frozen in amber. The brass spittoon in the corner, the cockeyed hat tree and the wobbly table cluttered with stacks of tattered *Field and Stream* magazines, as if we, Willy Witherspoon's customers, were all ardent fly fishermen and duck hunters, or as if, after our haircuts, we'd be going out gunning for a grizzly. Willy Witherspoon himself, with his soft ironic sweet smile and shiny bald head, his rimless glasses snowy with dandruff flakes, snipping, snipping, while the pitter-patter flowed out of him.

I got up in the chair and Willy Witherspoon twinkled at me and tapped his comb twice with his scissors. Then he started snipping and my curls began falling onto the floor.

The sleigh bells on the barbershop door jingled and Bill Rassmussen, the town cop, walked in.

"How's everything downtown today, Bill?"

"Pretty good, Willy. Pretty good." Bill Rassmussen sank into a chair and picked up a *Field and Stream*. "The meatloaf is on special down at the diner, Willy."

"The meatloaf, Bill? The meatloaf, you say?"

"Yep, that's right, Willie. They got the meatloaf today."

Back at the house, by way of further smoothing things over, I gave my sister the Civil War diary Aunt Mizpah had sent to me in New York, along with the twins' Virginia Rose child's tea set. Then we had another confab at the tulip bed, near the graves of our little pets, Tippy and Mittens.

"I'm sorry about the things I said," my sister began.

"No worries. You were right."

"You look nice, by the way. Like a regular Cooperstown guy."

"Well, I am one, you know."

For old time's sake we walked over to the Frog Hollow Grocery Market and bought orange Popsicles.

"I wonder if Mad Lucy's still around?" I ventured.

"Nope," Erin said. "They carted her off to Binghamton. Oh, it was years ago. Didn't you hear?"

"No, I guess…I've been sort of…out of touch."

"Thanks for the children's tea set, by the way," Erin said as we started back to the house. "You know, actually seeing the teacups, touching them, handling them, makes the whole business about the Paris Green and the picnic under the elms seem much more real. I can almost hear Grandma Maddalyn whispering, '*Drink your tea, my Pretties.*' I don't know if I believe the story about the tree being struck by lightning, but I'd like to believe it. I want to believe that it's true."

"Me too."

"Oh, and guess what… Sparky D'Onofrio made it to the Senate. You remember Sparky D'Onofrio? Most Likely To Succeed? It's Senator D'Onofrio now. Can you believe that?"

"I believe it."

The church bells began to ring and then the five o'clock whistle blew down at the Sawmill and every dog in town began to howl, a distant crazy chorus of yodeling whoops.

"By the way, Lummy Haverhill's dead. Kicked in the head by a horse."

"Lummy Haverhill… My God. A Cooperstown icon."

"At least it was quick. He never knew what hit him."

13

Back in New York once again I tried to work on my screenplay, but somehow it all seemed lifeless and empty and dead. I peered into the Angels Camp Tavern, deserted except for Tequila Lil, hunched alone at the bar, muttering through her bad teeth and waving an imaginary baton, the conductor of an invisible orchestra.

But at least the wedding had been a great success. My mother's side of the family, the German side—that coterie of cold Prussians—was represented only by Aunt Mizpah, who had always seemed to me somehow to be more of a Mulvaney than a Shimmersalz.

In fact, I'd taken my father's car and picked Aunt Mizpah up at the bus station in Oneonta. She looked much younger than I remembered, even though I hadn't seen her since I was a child. And I soon learned the reason. After all these years, Aunt Mizpah, too, was getting married! Her intended was a local man, a Brandon man, an executive with the Ayrshire Breeders Association, a widower with two grown daughters. Aunt Mizpah and her fiancé had met at a picnic at Lake Dunmore.

And the Mulvaneys? *Hurrah for the Mulvaneys!* Truly, the Mulvaneys had their day. Everyone was there. My father, Rufus, and Aunt Livia and my grandfather Sean Mulvaney, the railroad brakeman from Oneonta, my grandmother Effigale Alice Mulvaney, and Uncle Harry and Aunt Grace from Milford, and dozens more who crawled out of the woodwork.

The Mulvaneys, a tribe of gluttons and drunkards. Rooting and rollicking, snouting up turnips and truffles. Lips like funnels, sucking up the swill. Here's Aunt Elsie, big as a barrel, with her piglets stuck to her dugs like lovely little sausages. Thomas O'Malley from Whigs Corners, a frightful old rummy, in my mother's words, gorging and guzzling with swinish glee. Little Jimmy Moriarity—Little Jimmy with the watch eye—crocked to his pig-whiskers: *"Good slop!"* And dear old Uncle Harry, waggling his curly tail, snorkeling down a generous helping of hog-fodder.

Hurrah, then, hurrah for the Mulvaneys, wine guzzlers and good trenchermen all! May they live and prosper and prevail!

What now, Pilgrim? I was broke once again. Hal had gone back to sea, to gain more experience, and I had no tools and precious little inclination to pursue the idiot work he and I had been doing with the sheetrock and the painting. Brenda was in Broken Bow, getting sober or getting drunk. I was at loose ends. I got a call from Roddy. He was off the sauce, attending meetings with Big Joe, and he was running again to El Paso and Laredo and Brownsville. And Chubby wanted me back.

But I had one more dove hidden in my cape, or so I thought. If I couldn't finish the screenplay in New York, maybe I could do it in Vermont. Aunt Mizpah, at my sister's wedding, was in a jolly mood and she'd invited me to come, spend a month, and be on hand for her nuptials in mid-October. I borrowed thirty dollars from the bartender at the Angels Camp Tavern, packed my things and caught the Greyhound to Brandon.

In the kitchen of the old house at 61 Park Street, Aunt Mizpah handed me a corkscrew with a wooden handle and a bottle of Widmer's Lake Country Pink. We sat outside in the arbor, surrounded by grape leaves and lilac blossoms, and Aunt Mizpah started a fire in the stone barbeque.

"I thought we'd fix some hamburgers later on."

We talked about the old days at Lake Dunmore, where Aunt Mizpah's first fiancé, Ashley Van Deerlin, had drowned the day before their wedding. After two more bottles of Lake Country Pink, Aunt Mizpah went into the house and returned with Ashley Van Deerlin's photograph and his poems and love letters tied with a crinkly lavender bow. She put everything down on the firebricks and poked at the flames with a stick. Suddenly an impulse struck me and I got my half-finished screenplay, "Angels Camp," out of my gym bag and tossed that on the fire too.

"A toast!" Aunt Mizpah ventured, raising her wine glass. *"The Bonfire of the Vanities!"*

"Savonarola!"

"I guess we've both turned a corner, Jerzy. What about New York?"

"I'm not going back. It's a great place, but—"

"You wouldn't want to live there! You'll write, Jerzy."

"Sure, Aunt Mizpah. To you, always."

"Yes, but I mean—"

"Oh, that. Yeah, sure. Only no more screenplays!"

I called Roddy and we arranged to meet—not in Clear Lake since Maryann was on the warpath—but at the Bosselman Truck Stop in Altoona, about a hundred miles south of Clear Lake.

Two days later I met Roddy at Bosselman's off I-35 at 4:00 a.m. after sleeping most of the way on the bus. We had a lot to talk about, but there'd be plenty of time for that on the road. Roddy had our running money in an envelope.We both ordered the absurdly large "Truckers Special Breakfast"—three eggs, ham and bacon, home fries with sausage gravy, and buttermilk biscuits. And coffee, of course. We loaded up on coffee.

It was getting light in the east when we walked out to our rig with our coffees. We had forty-five thousand pounds of fertilizer for Terre Haute, and then we'd be pulling a load of corn down to Del Rio.

"Boy, that's ripe." I'd forgotten just how sharp, how penetrating, how invasive the aroma of sun-dried, pulverized cow shit can be.

"You'll get used to it." Roddy slapped the dust out of his Powder River Stetson. "Listen, do you mind driving first? I had to run up to Savage with a load of corn last night. No sleep."

"Sure, no problem."

The other guys were lined up out there, parked on either side of our rig, Schneider, Werner, England, J.B. Hunt, and the bedbug haulers, Mayflower, Atlas, Bekins, and all of them idling, their engines turning over, a steady roar like a single living organism.

We climbed up into the cab. I got behind the wheel. Roddy finished his coffee and began taking off his boots.

"I wonder if Marisa and Evita are still at the Addita Club."

"I guess we'll find out."

Roddy dived into the sleeper.

I fastened my seat belt, checked my mirrors, found second gear and released the brakes. Roddy pulled back the sleeper curtain and poked his head out. "Keep it between the ditches, okay?"

ABOUT THE AUTHOR

Donald O'Donovan was born in Cooperstown, New York. A teenage runaway, he rode freights and hitchhiked across America, served in the US Army with the 82nd Airborne Division, lived in Mexico, and worked at more than 200 occupations including telephone psychic, undertaker and roller skate repairman. A former long distance truck driver, he wrote *Confessions of a Bedbug Hauler* while running 48 states and Canada for Schneider National. As a volunteer at the Braille Institute in Los Angeles he recorded several western novels, and subsequently studied voice acting with James Alburger and Penny Abshire. O'Donovan lived for two years at the historic Wilshire Royale Hotel while writing *Tarantula Woman* (Open Books, 2011), and wrote the first draft of *Night Train* (Open Books, 2010) on 23 yellow legal pads while homeless in the streets of LA. An optioned screenwriter and voice actor with film and audio book credits, Donald O'Donovan lives mostly in Los Angeles.